NEVER SAY PIE

LEXY BAKER COZY MYSTERY SERIES BOOK 14

LEIGHANN DOBBS

SUMMARY

When the president of the Brook Ridge Falls Senior
Center Book Club is found dead, facedown in one of the
pies meant for the club's pie-eating contest, Lexy and
her posse of iPad-toting grandmothers take it upon
themselves to find the killer. Too bad the only potential
clue might be buried inside one of the many pies taken
by the police for evidence.

That's no problem. Lexy, Nans, and the ladies will
use their uncanny methods of deduction to ferret out the
killer. They waste no time filling their suspect list.

Was it the crusty old author?

The flaky antiques dealer?

The cheating husband with his half-baked grief act?

They all had means, motive, and opportunity and
seem to be harboring secrets. But what has Lexy really
worried is that someone in her group seems to have a
secret of her own.

Just when the case seems impossible to solve, they
come across another clue. Will Lexy and her posse
realize its hidden meaning before it's too late?

CHAPTER ONE

Summer at the Brook Ridge Retirement Community had never looked so festive. Pastel paper streamers draped from the ceiling, and foil balloons and fresh flowers decorated the center of the twenty or so round tables for eight placed around the main dining room.

The savory smell of roast beef mingled with the sweet scent of pie crust, and the din of conversation punctuated by cutlery clinking on plates permeated the air. The annual Book Club Gala was in full swing, and Lexy Baker and her assistant, Cassie, were catering the event.

"Did you put out the apple and cherry yet?" Lexy asked Cassie as she surveyed the crowded room, her heart swelling with pride at the way people were stuffing their plates at the buffet table. Lexy ran a bakery, but this was the first event at which she was catering the whole meal. By the looks of the way people were going up for seconds—and some for thirds —it was a huge success.

But the main attraction of the gala was the pie-eating contest that had yet to start. That was the part Lexy was most nervous about. Twenty contestants would be gobbling up her homemade pies, and she hoped they were good enough for them to want to keep eating a whole pie. "What about the blueberry and coconut cream?"

"Stop being such a worrywart," Cassie teased, her magenta-tipped spiked hair blazing brightly beneath the overhead lights, a vast array of rings lining each of her ears, the gems glistening each time she moved her head. "Just one more trip to the pie room, and we should be set."

Lexy and Cassie had been best friends since grade school, but that wasn't the only reason Lexy had hired Cassie as her assistant at her bakery, The Cup and Cake. Not only was Cassie loyal and trustworthy, but she made a mean icing, and some of her cake designs were better than Lexy's. She was also attentive, upbeat, and hardworking. Tonight, Cassie was in charge of transferring the freshly baked pies into the room where the contest would be held so they could cool.

Lexy had initially hoped to cool them in the kitchen windows or maybe even at tables under the windows in the pie room, but Mary Archer, the community center president, had put the kibosh on that. She wanted the windows to remain locked for security reasons. So Lexy had had to make do with making sure the pies were taken out early enough to be the perfect temperature for the contest. Combined with the fact that they were also baking pies for the desserts of the guests who were not in the contest, it made for one complicated setup. Not to worry—Lexy could handle complicated, especially with Cassie at her side.

"Great. Thanks."

While Cassie scooted off to finish setting up in the pie room, as they'd taken to calling it, Lexy stood off to the side to figure out what to do next. The list seemed endless. They had to clear the dirty dishes from the tables, check the buffet table to make sure all the chafing dishes were still operating and full, and start cleaning up the kitchens. So much to do, so little time.

Okay, gotta start with something. Lexy spun around to head toward the buffet and collided with a sign propped on an easel. *Ooops.*

She caught the large piece of cardboard before it crashed to the floor. It was the sign for the pie-eating contest announcing the grand prize, a signed first edition of *The Catcher in the Pie*, a cozy mystery written by famed author Chandler Bennington. The guy had been writing for ages, since the 1970s, according to the bio under his photo, and his books featured an amateur sleuth who owned a pie bakery. Considering Lexy owned her own bakery, she felt a sudden affinity for this sleuth, even if she hadn't actually read any of Bennington's books. *Never any extra time to sit down for a few hours with a novel and good glass of wine these days.*

Lexy nodded to several residents of the retirement complex who walked past, giving her strange glances as she battled with the sign. She knew most of them because her grandmother, Mona Baker—or Nans, as Lexy called her—was a well-known resident.

Near the front of the large conference room, the microphone squawked as the president of the community's book club, Mary Archer, tapped it. The din stopped while people glanced at the stage and covered their ears. It started right up again as Mary launched into her introductory speech. Not many of the residents seemed to be paying much attention, continuing to eat or walking away to join the gambling in one of the conference rooms that had been arranged with poker tables. Still, Mary kept talking, droning on about how she'd found the signed copy of Bennington's book at a rummage sale and she'd saved it for months until this party because she thought it would make the perfect prize.

Finally, she put away the paper she'd been reading from and cleared her throat. The mic screeched with feedback, gaining everyone's attention again, along with a few disgruntled glares. Her next words, though, had the entire community center perking up.

"And I'm also thrilled to announce that we have a very special guest with us today, ladies and gentlemen. It's my great pleasure to introduce the author himself, Chandler Bennington, who has graciously taken time out of his busy schedule to travel here to New Hampshire to be with us today." She gestured to a man standing off to the side in baggy brown trousers and a rather worn-looking cardigan. If someone had asked Lexy to conjure an image of a crusty old writer, it would be Bennington—tousled gray hair sticking up at odd angles around his head, eyes hidden behind thick glasses, shoulders slightly rounded from too much time behind a computer, and hands shoved in his pockets. At Mary's introduction, he seemed to withdraw further into the shadows, if that were possible. "It was quite a coup getting Mr. Bennington here to present his book. He rarely makes appearances, but I'm nothing if not persistent."

Low snickers ran through the crowd.

Mary, who was also president of the community center association, took the author's reticence in stride and quickly covered the disappointment in her expression. She'd obviously been expecting more of a response from him, maybe a bow or wave or something, but got nothing in return. Mary forced her smile back into place and continued without missing a beat. "Wonderful. Let's give the caterers time to clear the tables and ourselves a chance to move around and work off some of that food. Then we'll get started with the pie-eating contest in about twenty minutes. Thank you again, everyone, for attending."

Lexy jumped into action and grabbed a large round tray from near the wall where she'd stashed it earlier. She began making the rounds, loading glasses and flatware and plates.

When she filled one tray, she set it off in the corner of the room before returning with a fresh one. The kitchens were down the hall, so it was more efficient to gather everything first before hauling it all back there later. Catering was hard work and good exercise. It also was a great way to expand her business. Plus, it was fun to get out and see different places and people for a change. Of course, most of the people here were familiar to Lexy, especially the table of women whose plates she was clearing at the moment.

"Well, I'm not surprised Mary came across that book at a rummage sale. Rumor has it she wastes so much time at those things that her house looks like a hoarder's paradise."

Lexy glanced over at the speaker, her grand-mother. She was perched on the edge of her chair, scraps of ham and mashed potatoes on her plate. Seated around the table was her group of friends, all leaning in toward each other for post dinner gossip.

"And that author. I've heard he's no better than a recluse. Look at him. Talk about something the cat dragged in."

"Nans!" Lexy said, reaching past her to clear a pile of plates. "That's not very nice."

"True, though, dear," Nans's friend Ida said. She was a small woman with twinkling blue eyes and a devious grin. Her choice of blouse today was quite apropos, with tiny books in various shades of green and blue patterned all over the fabric. "And I can't imagine where he got the ideas for those crazy stories of his. I mean, really, who could imagine a bakery owner stum-

LEIGHANN DOBBS

bling across dead bodies all the time? It's preposterous."

Lexy fumbled a glass on the table but managed to catch it before anything spilled. The truth was, Lexy and the ladies tended to run into more than their fair share of trouble through the bakery and associated catering events—dead bodies included. Not that any of the elder ladies were shocked about this. Quite the opposite. Nans and her cohorts thrived on investigating murders. They'd taken to hiring themselves out as the Ladies' Detective Club. They'd even helped Lexy's husband, police detective Jack Perillo, on a few cases.

Helen gave one of her usual dismissive snorts. She looked as if she were stuck back in the Jackie-O days, with her perfect, demure dress and immaculate silver bobbed hair. She shrugged and shook her head, her tone clipped. "It's completely ridiculous."

Lexy continued clearing plates, noticing that everyone at the table except Helen had eaten their dessert. Her slice of pecan pie still sat before her.

"Don't you like pecan, Helen? What kind do you like? I'll grab you a slice of whatever you want," Lexy offered.

"No, thank you." Helen straightened in her chair.

She was so stiff that Lexy thought her spine might snap. "I'm off pastry for now. Low-carb diet."

Even as she spoke, she kept eyeing Ida's slice of cherry pie. There was also a plate of pastries from the buffet table within reach. Lexy wasn't sure about Helen, but *she'd* sure be tempted by the items on the plate.

Ida chuckled. "Eh, go ahead and have one, Helen. No one's watching. It's a special occasion anyway."

"No." Helen shook her head emphatically. "I've joined the Low-Carb Dieters Club, and that Rena Wakowski is like a drill sergeant with us. She's sitting right over there, and if she sees me, I'll never hear the end of it. I don't want to get into trouble. Besides, I've already lost ten pounds, and I intend to keep it off."

"Well, that was fun!" Ruth, another of Nans's friends, tossed a wad of cash on the table, pulled out a seat, and then dropped into her chair. "Been playing poker at the tables next door. Won a bundle!" She stacked her bills neatly. "Good thing I left before that Rena Wakowski took it all, though. She's nothing but a card shark, that one. As sharp as a tack too!"

"Probably because of her low-carb lifestyle," Helen said, sounding superior. "It's been scientifically shown to improve the memory, and card games like poker are all about remembering which cards were played and which are still in the deck."

Ruth gave her a skeptical look. "If you say so. But I still prefer my pie, thanks." She took a large bite of her apple-rhubarb and grinned at Helen, who rolled her eyes.

"Did you guys get a load of Carol Newburg over there?" Nans said, turning the ladies' attention back to the party. "Talk about an attention hound. She's about as overdressed as you can get. This is a book club party, not the Oscars. A red floor-length gown. Ugh."

Ida laughed around a mouthful of cherry filling, a glob dripping onto her chin. "You think that's bad—what about Hazel Martin?" She cocked her head toward the opposite side of the room and pointed with her fork. "Looks like she didn't even bother to change at all. I'm pretty sure she's still wearing her bathrobe from this morning. Methinks another visit to the staff psychologist might be in order soon."

Lexy bit back a smile and continued loading the tray with dishes. She hoped she was as active and happy as the ladies were when she got to be Nans's age.

Lexy felt someone push her and turned to see a woman had accidentally bumped into her.

"Oh, excuse me," the woman said then scurried

over to one of the tables. She slipped a piece of paper beneath one of the dinner plates before hurrying on her way. Lexy had seen her around the community center before, usually hanging around with Mary or the other board members, but had never met her.

"Well, how do you like that?" Nans said, staring after the brunette as she scuttled away. "What do you think that was all about?"

"Got me," Lexy said, collecting used flatware. "I don't even know who that was."

"Sylvia Hensel." Ruth's tone was hushed. "She's the treasurer around here and has her pulse on all the happenings at the center, if you know what I mean. And I wonder what she was doing at that table. I think that plate is where Howard Archer was sitting."

Lexy glanced over at the empty spot. "Maybe it's for the door prizes. Perhaps he's won. Have they had the raffles yet?"

"Not that I've heard," Helen said. "And shouldn't the committee have taken care of all that before this started?"

Ida lifted her plate of cherry pie to look underneath. "Nope. No note here."

Everyone lifted their plates to check and shook their heads.

Nans lifted the plates at the two empty seats. "No notes under any of them."

"Hey, no one ever accused Sylvia of being the brightest bulb in the lamp," Ruth added. "Wouldn't surprise me if she left it to the last minute."

"And did you see what she was wearing?" Nans craned her neck to keep the woman in her sights. "Just look at that gaudy pearl necklace and those enormous pearl earrings. Goodness, she wears them every single day."

"She told me once they were her mother's," Helen said. "She goes on and on about how they're antique and quite valuable."

This time it was Ruth's turn to snort. "Lorelei Summers says those pearls are worthless. Not even real. They're cheap fakes! And she should know, being the local antiques dealer and all."

Lexy finished clearing Nans's table then moved to the head table at the front of the room. The guest of honor, Chandler Bennington, sat there alone, staring at the centerpiece. Lexy noticed that he had no dessert plate in front of him. Feeling a bit sorry for the guy, she gave him a kind smile. "Hello, Mr. Bennington. I notice you don't have any pie. If you'd tell me what kind you prefer, I'll be happy to bring you a slice."

"Oh." He glanced up, seemingly distracted. "Pecan."

"Sure thing." Lexy rushed back to the buffet table, where the extra slices were kept, and grabbed a fresh piece of pecan pie and a clean fork and a napkin before hurrying back to the main dining room to deliver it. She set it in front of him, expecting perhaps a thank-you, but no dice. Ah well. You learned to roll with the punches in the service business. "Enjoy!"

He stared at the food as if it were a poisonous viper, keeping his hands firmly clenched in his lap. Bennington mumbled something under his breath Lexy didn't quite catch then pushed away from the table, bumping into her in the process. He headed for the bar in the far corner. He didn't even touch the pie she'd gone to all that trouble to get for him. *Talk about ungrateful.* Fine! If he preferred the bar to her pie, then so be it. She knew that plenty of others liked her pie just fine, judging by the way the slices were disappearing from the dessert table.

Lexy sighed and continued her cleanup duties, thinking all those rumors about Bennington being a crotchety old goat might be true. He put his fictional heroine in jeopardy by having her investigate dead bodies all the time, but if the characters in his books ever got a load of the author's personality, it would be more than enough to scare them.

"Lexy," Cassie said, coming up beside her, "want to take a last check of the pie room with me to make sure it's ready to go?"

"Sure." Lexy looked across the room at the clock on the wall behind the buffet table. If things were running on time, the contest was due to start soon. Lexy hefted the last full tray on her shoulder and headed back toward the corner to drop it off. As she weaved through the tables, she spotted Chandler Bennington arriving at the bar set up near the entrance. Beyond was the hallway leading to the kitchens and the administrative offices. The pie room was down there too, where Cassie had placed the pies when they came out of the ovens in the kitchen. It was nothing more than a small space with long tables and seats set up for the contestants. Nothing fancy, but it would do the trick.

Before looking away again, Lexy spotted Helen standing near the side of the doorway to the main dining room, clutching her purse to her chest with a furtive expression. That was odd. Helen usually looked nothing less than regal. Then again, she'd seen Helen do some pretty odd things these past couple of years, many times in cahoots with Nans and the other ladies.

They were probably up to one of their schemes. Lexy didn't have time to ask. She was in a hurry, and now wasn't the time to dawdle. The pie-eating contest was starting any minute, and she needed to check the pie room. Her reputation as a caterer, not to mention as a baker, was on the line.

As Lexy dropped off the tray, she spotted Ruth standing near the end of the buffet table. She was bent over, looking under the warming tray, a large metal spoon covered in scalloped potatoes held high in her hand. Darn, had the burner under the chafing dish gone out again? Ruth was going to light the place on fire.

Lexy hurried over. "I've got it, Ruth." She whipped some matches out of her pocket and lit the burner.

"Thank you, dear. These potatoes are a bit cold—might want to heat them up in the kitchen or something."

A motion in the hallway caught Lexy's eye. It was Cassie tapping her watch. Yikes! The pie room!

"Will do, Ruth." Lexy rushed off toward Cassie.

Some of her stress must've shown on her face, because Cassie asked, "What's wrong?"

"Nothing. I just want this contest to go perfectly.

It's the first event we've catered here for Mary, so I want it to run smoothly." Lexy sighed. "Listen to me; you'd think it was my first event. I'm sure it will all be fine."

"Better than fine. I'm sure it'll be wonderful. Don't worry so much. I've got your back."

Down at the end of the hall, the lights in the pie room were still off. That was on purpose, as they didn't want anyone getting an early look at the pies. Lexy peered in. She could make out the two long L-shaped banquet tables, each table set with ten chairs.

In front of each chair sat a whole pie. White linen tablecloths covered the tables, the same as in the main dining room, and the same streamers and foil balloons decorated the space. Along one side of the room, a row of sheer-curtained windows allowed enough filtered sunlight in to cast long shadows over the tables. A curtain fluttered slightly, drawing Lexy's attention, and she realized with a start that someone was sitting in the last seat.

Darn it! Was someone cheating ... thinking they could get a head start on the contest?

"Excuse me!" Lexy yelled as she started toward the figure. "The contest hasn't started yet. We'll have to ask you to leave the room, or you'll be disqualified."

No response. She came to a stop next to the

person. Something wasn't right. The woman had her face in the pie, but...

Lexy tapped her shoulder. "Excuse me."

The body in the chair tipped sideways and crashed to the floor, splashing blueberry filling everywhere.

Cassie gasped. "Oh my gosh!"

"Turn on the lights!" Lexy crouched, pressing her fingers to the woman's neck, noticing the dark red smudges on the contest trophy on the floor beside the body. Cherry pie filling... or something else? Blinking hard in the sudden illumination, she peered through the muck of pie filling on the woman's face.

It was Mary Archer, and Lexy didn't even need to search for a pulse to know that Mary was definitely dead.

CHAPTER TWO

The police arrived in a blaze of sirens and blue lights a short time later, Lexy's husband, Jack Perillo, and Cassie's husband, John Darling, included. They were both homicide detectives in Brook Ridge Falls. That was about where the similarities between them ended, though. Jack was ruggedly handsome with tanned skin, honey-brown eyes, and dark, close-cropped hair. John was taller and rangier, with longish blond hair and pale-blue eyes. He was handsome too but in a different way from Jack. In addition to being partners, the two were also the best of friends.

"Are you okay?" Jack's brown eyes were soft with concern that melted Lexy's heart as he took her aside for questioning.

"I'm fine. I mean I've found bodies before." Lexy was no stranger to discovering a dead body. Of course, it was always a shock but still not nearly as upsetting as the first time.

"Okay, then stay put. I have some things to take care of, then I'll need to ask you some questions."

Cassie and Lexy stood off to the side and watched as the police went about their business. They'd asked everyone to remain until they could get names and numbers. One officer was going through the guests, doing just that. Nans, Ida, Ruth, and Helen were seated at their table, talking in hushed whispers, their eagle eyes watching everything.

After about twenty minutes, Jack came back and got them. He led Lexy and Cassie back to the pie room, and they went over every detail of how they'd discovered the body. The medical examiner had taken the body, but there was a spot on the floor where Mary Archer had fallen, now outlined with tape. The messy blueberry filling had crusted on the white linen tablecloth and the carpet. That would leave a stain, Lexy was sure.

She and Cassie reenacted exactly how they'd discovered the body and answered Jack's questions, then after a supportive squeeze of her upper arm, Jack left to talk to more people.

Nans, Ruth, Ida, and Helen had been hovering in the doorway. They made a beeline to Lexy and Cassie as soon as they were free from the police. Not a surprise—Lexy knew that Nans and the ladies would be conducting their own investigation.

The police were still photographing and putting down little yellow crime scene markers, so Nans pulled them back into the main dining area and sat them at a table before starting her interrogation.

"What happened after you discovered Mary's body?" Nans asked, her green eyes dancing with excitement.

"We secured the area, called the police, then announced the pie-eating contest was canceled, obviously." Lexy swallowed hard to cover the tremble in her body. "Why?"

"Did you see any clues?" Ida asked.

"No." Lexy exhaled, doing her best to remember exactly what she'd seen. She knew from experience that it was futile to discourage them. Nans and the ladies were going to investigate no matter what. And while this had caused some problems between Jack and her in the past, she kind of got the feeling now that he was on board with her helping Nans investigate as long as she didn't put herself in danger. "Just poor Mary Archer with her face stuck in a pie."

"Well, how did she die?" Helen asked. "Shot? Stabbed?"

"Maybe it was a heart attack," Ida suggested.

"She could have been clubbed," Cassie spoke up, earning raised brows from Nans and the ladies. Cassie didn't usually help with the investigations, but judging by the eager look on her face, Lexy knew she was not averse to pitching in.

"Why do you say that, dear?" Nans asked.

"That big old trophy was lying beside her," Cassie said.

"Oh ... that thing was heavy. It would make a great murder weapon," Ida said.

"Let's not jump to conclusions. She could have just been placing it in the room in preparation for the contest." Nans had already taken her iPad from her gigantic purse and was typing notes.

Ida leaned sideways in her chair to scowl down the hallway outside the entrance. Several officers tromped by with pies in their hands, apparently confiscating them for evidence. "Do they have to take them all? What a waste of good pie!"

"Who cares about pie when we've got a murder to investigate?" Nans said, all but rubbing her hands together with glee. "I wonder who could've killed Mary."

"Not sure." Ruth's dark eyes glinted with excitement. "There were a lot of people at the party. Anyone could've slipped in there without being noticed."

Helen hung back a bit, unusually quiet, not commenting at all as she still clutched that purse of hers to her chest. It was a nice bag but nothing to be so possessive about.

"Let's think back," Nans said, putting her dogged logic to work. "Who was doing what right before Lexy came down the hallway and discovered the body?"

"Well, I was finishing clearing the tables of dirty dishes." Lexy frowned, unable to stop herself from participating. She was sure Jack wouldn't mind because the murder had taken place in the community center, practically the ladies' backyard. She went on with what she knew, telling them the same thing she'd already told the police. Jack wouldn't mind that, would he? It was mostly public knowledge. "I remember checking the clock because I wanted to make sure the pie room was ready for the contest. It was seven fifteen. That was maybe five minutes before we found Mary because I had to detour to the buffet table to light the burners under the scalloped potatoes."

Nans typed all this in as the ladies chattered amongst themselves, but Helen still remained silent. What was wrong with her? Maybe she was upset about Mary's death. Had she known Mary well? Lexy had never heard her mention being close to the Archers, but then she didn't really know all of the ladies' friends. Still, she did look awfully pale. She'd barely touched her food at the table, even the things without carbs. Could it be her new low-carb diet wasn't agreeing with her?

"If I've learned anything in my years of sleuthing, the spouse is normally suspect numero uno." Nans glanced over her shoulder toward where Howard Archer was now being questioned by the police. The poor man looked upset. Perhaps *too* upset. He looked to be in his midseventies, had neatly trimmed dark-gray hair and a mustache, and wore glasses. His brown outfit made him look about as threatening as a church mouse. He didn't really look like a cold-blooded killer, but then most murderers didn't.

Ida shrugged. "Mary was good friends with Sylvia Hensel, wasn't she? Maybe we should ask her about it. Bet she could shed some light on their marital situation."

"Ladies," Jack said, coming back over to the group after finishing up with Howard. He caught Lexy's eye and gave her a small smile and wink before resuming his usual stoic work face. He must have known what they were talking about. Did this mean he approved?

"I'd like to ask you all a few questions, if you don't mind."

"What?" Nans nudged Jack in the side with her elbow. She and Jack got on like gangbusters when she wasn't sticking her nose into his cases. "No dire warnings today about staying out of police business?" she joked.

"That still applies, Mona," Jack said, flipping open his notepad and giving her a stern look, which didn't fool anyone, least of all Nans. "But I do have questions I'm hoping you ladies can help with. Do any of you know who might want Mary Archer dead?"

"No," Ruth said, her tone too eager. "But we can find out."

Jack shook his head, his lips tightening slightly. "I don't want any of you to put yourselves in danger. Understand? Murder is serious business." He looked up again and met Lexy's eyes briefly before looking back at Nans. "But this time I'll make a slight exception. I'm hoping that because this happened right here in your retirement center, you ladies might have access to information and sources that I don't. People tend to clam up when the police ask the questions. So, if you do happen to hear anything, I'd appreciate knowing. Not that I'm asking you to go out of your way to find out, but if information becomes available within the normal course of conversation, I'd love to know."

"Right." Nans gave him a conspiratorial grin. "Normal course."

Lexy couldn't help thinking about how the close relationship Jack shared with Nans and her friends had changed over the years. Jack had started out as Nans's neighbor. The two had developed a friendship despite the difference in age, and Nans had spent quite a bit of effort trying to fix Lexy up with him. Lexy had resisted, but eventually, Nans had sold her house to Lexy, making Lexy and Jack become neighbors. Of course, the romance didn't start until Lexy ended up as Jack's number-one suspect in a murder, but that was all in the past.

"What about me?" Lexy asked, nudging him with her shoulder. "Do I have permission to snoop too?"

"As long as you stay safe, honey," he said and dropped a quick kiss on her cheek. And boy, wasn't that a far cry from the last case he'd wrapped up a few months earlier. She'd almost promised never to investigate again. Good thing that hadn't happened. Lexy enjoyed investigating almost as much as baking. Besides, her grandmother wasn't going to stop, and someone had to make sure Nans didn't put herself in danger.

Jack finished questioning them while John talked to Cassie. By then, the uniformed officers had finished with the crime scene and were sending everyone home. Jack excused himself, and John hugged Cassie before both men headed back to the station.

Nans was still excited. "Get your rest tonight, ladies. We can start our investigation fresh first thing in the morning."

Everyone nodded at Nans except Ida, whose eyes were glued to the officers carrying out the last of the pies. "We'd better hurry. The sooner we find out who the killer is, the sooner the police will release those pies."

CHAPTER THREE

*L*exy stayed at the community center, cleaning up, long after everyone else had left. Thankfully, the police did not have the kitchen cordoned off, so she was able to wash the dishes and pack up the rest of the food. When she returned home, haggard and tired, it was almost midnight. She pushed open the door and was greeted by the clicking of tiny nails on hardwood and a flurry of white fur. Sprinkles, her half shih tzu, half poodle, flew into her arms and licked her face, causing Lexy to smile for the first time in hours.

Jack peeked out from the kitchen. "Hungry?"

"And tired." Lexy put Sprinkles down and started across the living room of the Craftsman-style bungalow. Nans had owned the house from the time she'd been married until she'd sold it to Lexy, and it held tons of happy childhood memories. Maybe someday she'd have a granddaughter to make similar happy memories with in this house, but right now, she and Jack were quite happy making their own memories.

Jack met her in the kitchen doorway, a tray filled with cutlery, bowls, a large salad, and most importantly, a bottle of wine. The smell of freshly baked rolls wafted out, and she lifted a gingham kitchen towel to reveal crusty golden rolls.

"Go relax on the couch. Figured you'd be hungry, so I made a chef salad and some buttermilk rolls."

Not for the first time, Lexy was reminded of one of the many reasons she'd married him. He was kind and thoughtful as well as good looking.

They ate on the couch, Sprinkles attentively watching every bite they took. The salad, rolls, and wine had a calming effect, and by the time they were done, Lexy had almost forgotten about the day's events.

She leaned back on the couch and put her head on Jack's sturdy shoulder. "So you seriously don't mind Nans and the ladies investigating?"

"Do you mean I don't mind *you* investigating?"

Jack teased. They both knew that if Nans was going to investigate, Lexy wouldn't be far behind. He settled back into his seat, cuddling her close again as he talked. "Well, I figured you ladies are going to investigate whether I say it's okay or not. This way, I can supervise and keep an eye on you. Besides, I was telling the truth earlier when I told Nans they might have access to information I won't on this case."

"That's true." Sprinkles snuggled deeper between them, causing Lexy to scoot over a bit to make room. "The ladies do know how to investigate."

"And they aren't hampered by following police protocol. Plus, people will talk more freely around them. Those older folks at the retirement community are a tight-knit bunch. They've been through world wars and the worst sorts of interrogations. Keeping to themselves is a way of life for a lot of them. They won't tell me anything they don't want to, and they certainly don't trust me because I'm not one of them. Your grandmother and her friends are. They have friends there, and friends talk. Just try to keep them on the straight and narrow, eh?'

"Me?" Lexy giggled into his warm chest. "Thanks for giving me that job. Trying to rein in Nans and her friends is like trying to wrangle cats." Sprinkles frowned up at Lexy at the word "cats," and Lexy scratched her behind the ear. "But I'll do my best. Let's compare notes. I'm dying to know what you and John found out today."

In the past, Lexy wouldn't have dared to ask. Jack had always seemed so unhappy when she poked into his cases, but after what he'd just explained, she could see he was okay with it this time. She'd long ago given up making assumptions about him. She'd learned her lesson a couple of months earlier when she'd jumped to the wrong conclusion that he'd been having an affair. It turned out he was just buying her a much-needed new car. Sweet, sweet man. So, honesty was her new best policy.

"Okay," he said before sipping his wine, his expression contemplative. "You go first. Did Mona and her friends come up with any good suspects after I left?"

"Not that I know of, but I think they plan to hit it hard tomorrow. Oh, wait. Ida did mention that Sylvia Hensel was good friends with Mary Archer and that she might be able to provide some insight on her marriage to Howard."

"Great. I'll make a note to talk to her again tomorrow, then." He drank some more wine. "Let me know if they find out anything else in the morning."

"Will do." She shifted to look up at him. "Okay. I

shared what I have, now tell me what you and John have found."

"Not much, unfortunately." Jack sighed. "The medical examiner said that the victim died from blunt force trauma to the head, most likely with the contest trophy. We checked it for prints at the scene but didn't find any. Too bad Mona and her friends didn't go snooping in that pie room today too."

"Yeah, Nans and her friends do see everything, don't they?" That got Lexy thinking about what she'd seen earlier in the dining room, with Helen near the hallway. The pie room was at the end of the hallway, but she must have told Jack she was there when he'd questioned her earlier, right? Or should she mention it? No. There was no sense getting poor Helen into trouble if she hadn't said anything to Jack. Especially because Lexy knew Helen couldn't have had anything to do with Mary's murder. She just must not have seen anything pertinent.

It was strange, though, because Jack had just said it was too bad *none* of them went snooping down there. Of course, just because Helen was in the hallway didn't mean she'd gone to the pie room. She probably had a perfectly logical explanation for being in the corridor that led to both the pie room and the kitchens.

Lexy shook off her thoughts and moved on to Ida

33

and her concern over the removal of all those pies. Laughing, Lexy said, "Ida was sure upset about all those pies being confiscated earlier."

"Doesn't surprise me." Jack grinned. "For such a little thing, she can really put away the food, huh?"

"Yep." Ida couldn't have been more than five feet tall and weighed less than one hundred pounds, but Lexy had seen her pack away a dozen cupcakes from her shop in a single sitting.

Jack hugged Lexy tighter and kissed the top of her head then tucked it beneath his chin. Sprinkles climbed out from between them and curled into a ball in Lexy's lap. "Well, you can tell Ida that we had to take them because I noticed that some of the pies had been messed with. I'm sure that must have happened during the murder. You didn't notice any of them being messed with while they were cooling, did you?"

"Messed with?" Lexy leaned back so she could look him in the eyes, more concerned about the pies being messed with than the fact that Jack actually knew the pies were cooling. She hadn't realized he'd paid that much attention to her baking. "How?"

"Like someone had dug around in the middle of them. Searching for something in there, perhaps? And on others, big hunks of the crusts were missing." He exhaled. "I'm sorry, honey. I know you worked really hard on them. But my guess is that maybe the killer dropped something into the pie when he hit Mary on the head. Then the killer rummaged around, trying to retrieve whatever it was. I know it's a long shot, but so far, it's the only clue we have, so I'm going with it."

CHAPTER FOUR

The next morning, Lexy dropped Sprinkles off at The Pampered Pooch for a bath and haircut and to have her nails clipped. The small pet grooming business was owned by Betty Farmer, who lived at the Brook Ridge Falls Retirement Community. Had she been at the party the previous night? Probably. Most of the residents had been, whether they were in the book club or not. Maybe Betty would have some information Lexy could use. But when Lexy arrived, she was told that Betty wasn't coming in until later that day. Oh well. Maybe that was for the best. If Lexy and the ladies discovered something today, perhaps she could use Betty to verify it.

After dropping off Sprinkles, Lexy stopped at The Cup and Cake long enough to make sure the coffee urns were perking, the cafe tables were sparkling clean, and the pastry case was full. She went over the plan for the day with Cassie then left her in charge and headed to the retirement center with a white bakery box full of fresh pastries. She knew Nans and the ladies would have their makeshift command center set up in Nans's dining room, and she didn't want to miss out on the review session.

She knocked on the apartment door then let herself in even before Nans called out, "Come in!"

Ida made a beeline for the pastry box, took it out of Lexy's hands, and lifted the lid to peer inside.

"Glad you could make it, Lexy. We were just about to go over the information we know. Grab a coffee and have a seat." Nans gestured at the mahogany dining table set with dainty cups and saucers and linen napkins. Ida was already placing the pastries on the triple-tiered server in the middle of the table. Naturally, she'd taken the liberty of piling a few of her favorites on her own plate.

Lexy sat across from Helen, who was looking rather grumpy. Her plate was empty, but she eyed everyone's pastries like a starving dog in a butcher shop. Maybe she was grumpy because her blood sugar was low.

Ida held out an apple turnover toward Helen. "Pastry?"

"You know I'm off carbs." Helen gave a snooty sniff, pulled a small container of fat-free cottage cheese from her handbag, and proceeded to open it. "Do any of you have any idea how many calories and carbs those pastries have in them? I mean, they look delicious, as always, but my health is more important. Why, did you know there's eleven grams of sugar alone just in that one apple turnover Ida's scarfing down?" She gave her friend a flat stare. "Eleven! Shameful. I much prefer my healthier alternative and less padding on my hips, thank you very much. No offense, Lexy."

"None taken." Lexy did her best not to laugh as Ida made a show of shoving half the turnover into her mouth at once just to tick Helen off. She chewed with a smile then wiped the crumbs from the front of her pastel floral-printed blouse, her gaze never leaving Helen.

"Good thing I didn't bring any gooey chocolate brownies or almond scones then, I guess," Lexy said.

"I'd love some of those too." Ida's tone was defiant. She crossed her arms and sat back. "A little extra padding never hurt anyone."

"As interesting as this topic is"—Nans cast an unamused stare at her friends—"I'd much prefer to hear if Jack spilled any investigation secrets to you last night, Lexy."

"Mmm, not really." Lexy finished the last bite of lemon Danish then wiped her mouth. They were exceptionally good today, she had to admit. The pastry dough was light and flaky with that hint of butter at the end, and the citrus filling was deliciously tart with a bit of sweet to keep you from puckering up completely. "Unfortunately, they just don't know much at this point. The only thing they did find out from the ME is that Mary was struck on the back of the head with the contest trophy. That's what killed her. But whoever committed murder just left it there on the floor."

"Did they get prints from the trophy?" Nans asked.

"Jack said no. It was wiped clean."

"Ah." Nans nodded sagely. "Premeditated, then."

"What about the pies?" Ida asked.

"Jack said they suspect someone lost something in one of them. That's why they took them all yesterday. He mentioned some looked like they'd been dug into in the middle, while others were missing large sections of crust."

Helen coughed around a bite of her cottage cheese and shifted in her seat, not looking at anyone.

"Darn." Ida sulked. "Now we'll never get them back to eat."

"Time to start mapping all this out." Nans rose and went into her spare bedroom then emerged with a large rolling whiteboard they used to keep track of clues and suspects. She opened a red marker, and the room filled with a noxious smell as she started writing, the marker squeaking on the board as she made several columns. At the top of each, she wrote titles—suspects, clues, and motives.

"Well, we can start by listing Howard Archer at the top of the suspects list," Ida said. "On all the TV shows, the spouse is always the first to be interrogated."

Nans wrote his name down then listed the trophy under clues. "I suppose it makes sense that the killer would use it, as it would've been handy. But then maybe that rules it out as a clue if it was only chosen because of convenience. And why would the killer leave it behind afterward?"

"Eh, leave it up there for now," Ruth chimed in. "My biggest concern is our lack of other suspects at the moment. Didn't anybody see anything suspicious right before Mary was killed?"

Ida frowned. "Honestly, that room was so busy right then I don't remember much of anything."

"Me either," Nans agreed. "So many people

milling about and things happening. The waiters, the speakers, and the committee members handling last-minute party business."

Lexy glanced at Helen, who was still scowling down into her cottage cheese, but didn't say anything. After all, what could she say? She'd seen her standing in the hallway near the main dining room entrance, looking a bit at odds. Hardly a crime. Given her strange behavior since she'd started her diet, not unusual. It just seemed strange that she wouldn't mention she was near the room. She was right at the end of the hallway just before Lexy found Mary's body. If she'd been in the hall, she might have seen the killer.

Of course, if Helen had seen anyone who could be the killer, she would say something. In all the chaos, it was possible Helen hadn't seen anything and there was nothing to mention. After all, she had seemed quite distracted by that handbag of hers. Lexy eyed the beige patent leather bag sitting on the floor next to Helen. Maybe it was filled with cottage cheese and she didn't want any of the other low-carb-ers to take her stash.

"I know!" Nans clapped her hands, making Lexy jump and drawing her attention back to the task at hand. "Helen, you still remember how to hypnotize people, yes? You could do that to us now to help us each remember what we saw at the exact time Mary Archer was killed."

"Oh, I don't know." Helen pushed aside her half-eaten cottage cheese cup. "I haven't done that in a long time. I'm out of practice."

"C'mon," Ida said. "It's probably like riding a bike. You never forget how."

"Yes, please." Ruth sat forward. "You can do me first."

Helen sighed. "Fine. But don't blame me if something goes wonky. You've been warned. I'm out of practice." She adjusted her seat and took Ruth's hand, tapping on the back of it lightly. "Okay, Ruth. I want you to close your eyes and relax. Concentrate only on the sound of my voice as all of your thoughts and cares start drifting away. That's it. Good." Her voice became lower, more melodic. "Yes. Perfect, Ruth. You are so relaxed now, floating in a warm pool of water. Nothing can hurt you. Nothing can harm you. Are you there with me?"

"Yes," Ruth said, her body sagging as her muscles went lax and her tone lightened to a whisper. "I'm there with you."

"Good." Helen nodded to Nans, who took over the questioning.

"Ruth, this is Mona. Can you remember back to the party yesterday? Can you tell me what you saw right before Lexy made her announcement about Mary Archer's murder?"

Ruth's brows drew together. "I remember playing poker in the gambling room next door, but then I got hungry. I came back into the main dining room to see if there was any leftover food on the tables, but the only thing I found were some cold scalloped potatoes." Her words were monotone. She frowned. "Those poker games went on all night. In the side rooms. I won even more money." Absently, she reached down and grabbed her purse from the floor near her chair and opened it to pull out a second huge wad of cash to match the first she'd showed them the day before. "I ... I don't remember anything else."

"Great." Helen brought Ruth out of her trance and then proceeded to put Ida under.

Ida, as expected, had been focused on the food. "I was watching the buffet table. It was on the side of the room. You had to pass it on the way to the hallway that led to the pie room."

"Did you notice anything amiss?" Nans asked.

"Yes!" Ida nodded. "Terribly amiss."

"What was it?" Nans asked, and they all leaned forward to hear her answer, anticipation thick in the air. Maybe they'd finally get a new suspect for Mary's murder.

"Anita Furbish," Ida said. "She went through that buffet line four times! And then she had the audacity to go back a fifth time to load up a plate with desserts. Then there was Jimmy O'Rourke! Why, he went through the prime rib station three times! Three! When there's a sign right there that clearly states there is a two-trips-per-person limit. Shameful!"

Nans rolled her eyes and shook her head. Everyone else sighed and sat back as Helen brought Ida out of her trance.

"This isn't quite working out as well as we'd hoped, is it?" Lexy asked.

"Never mind." Nans gave a dismissive wave. "Lexy, do you remember anything at all?"

Lexy looked over at Helen again then shook her head. What if Helen hypnotized Lexy and she spilled the beans on her secretive hallway maneuvers? That would be awkward. "No. I dropped off my last tray of dishes in the corner, then Cassie and I headed to the pie room to make sure everything was ready. That's when we found Mary." A shudder ran through Lexy at the remembrance of finding the body and the feel of that cool flesh beneath her fingertips when she'd felt for a pulse.

"We're getting nowhere fast with the suspect list, so let's move on to motive." Nans went back to scribbling on the whiteboard with that stinky dry-erase marker of hers. "What ideas do we have here?"

"Jealousy is always a good start," Helen said. "Greed or anger too."

"Which brings us back to the husband, Howard," Ida said.

"What about talking to Sylvia Hensel, as Ida mentioned yesterday?" Ruth asked. "She was good friends with Mary. They spent a lot of time in the office at the center together, and girls that work together tend to chat. She might know if something was amiss with their marriage."

"Good idea." Nans recapped the marker at last and set it back in the tray. "That's our plan today. Talk to Sylvia and find out what she knows about Mary's relationship with Howard."

"Let's go now." Nans turned to Lexy. "Do you have time to drive us?"

Lexy glanced at the cuckoo clock on Nans's wall. "I have a few hours to spare, but I have to pick Sprinkles up from the groomer's later on."

Nans's eyes lit up. "You mean Betty Farmer's place?"

"One and the same."

"Excellent. Betty was sitting at table five last night. She might have some insight."

"Perfect." Ida plucked an éclair off the tiered tray and jumped up from her seat. "Shouldn't take long to talk to Sylvia. Let's clean up and go."

After they cleaned up their mess, they set off from Nans's apartment building on the outskirts of the retirement complex to the community center club-house at its heart. It wasn't a long walk, but it was a scorcher of a day, already in the mideighties, and they decided it would be better to drive.

"Do you think she'll be there?" Lexy asked as they made their way to her new yellow VW bug parked in the lot next to the building. Just the sight of it sparkling in the morning sunshine made Lexy smile. It had been a gift from Jack to replace her previous VW that had become quite cantankerous.

"That's where she usually is about this time," Ruth said. "And today of all days, I'd think she'd be doing damage control, trying to keep everything straight after, well, you know, Mary's..."

You wouldn't think four senior citizens and one bakery owner would fit in a VW bug, but the ladies did yoga and were quite flexible, so it didn't take them long to squeeze into Lexy's car for the ride to the community center clubhouse.

CHAPTER FIVE

S ylvia Hensel was exactly where the ladies had predicted she'd be, buzzing around the community center like an agitated bee. Nans caught up with her outside the main office and convinced her to have a seat where they could all talk.

The center was quiet and empty and a little ominous given the police crime scene tape on the door to the pie room. Normally, there would be people about because there was usually a full calendar of activities, but apparently, people were avoiding the place after what had happened to Mary.

Nans chose a spot in the main room where they'd set up for dinner. All but one of the round tables had been folded and stacked along the wall. Lexy assumed the white tablecloths had been sent to the cleaners.

The long tables she'd set up for the buffet were gone too, rows of folded chairs stacked in their place. Today, with the silence and lack of people, it was quite a different vibe from the night of the party. More somber. Though Lexy thought the scent of roast beef and pie still lingered.

The carpet silenced their footsteps as they all pulled chairs around the one remaining table.

Lexy hadn't really paid much attention to Sylvia at the party. Mary had hired her to do the catering, and all the instructions at the event had come from her. This was the first time that Lexy was really getting a good look at Sylvia. She was a well-kempt woman, with dyed dark-brown hair cut and styled in a neat bob. Her makeup was light, and from the immovable expanse of her forehead, Lexy thought she might have had a few Botox injections. Diamond earrings glittered from her lobes, and she was clad in upscale-department-store garb. It looked as if Sylvia had the means to keep herself preserved for a long time to come. She kept a tissue clutched in her hand and frequently used it to dab the tears from her cheeks. With her other hand, she fiddled with the pearls around her neck.

"I'm sorry." She sniffled loudly once they were all seated. "I'm just so upset about what happened to poor Mary yesterday. I can't believe she's gone." More sniffling and dabbing with the tissue. "I had just been talking with her in the office shortly before she was killed." Sylvia shook her head, giving a visible shiver. "Mary said she had to ensure the caterers had everything they needed for the contest. She asked me to check on that cranky old Chandler Bennington while she did that, to make sure he was ready for his presentation and to get the bibs for the contest." Her voice caught on a sob. "I should have stopped her or gone with her. Maybe if I had, she'd still be alive. The police were just here, questioning me about all of this again, making me relive each awful moment."

"I'm so sorry for your loss, dear." Nans patted her hand gently, giving Lexy a quick glance as she did so. "I know you and Mary were good friends. Did you happen to see anyone else milling around the offices at the time Mary left you to check on the caterers?"

"No." Sylvia shrugged, frowning down at her hands clasped in her lap. "Well, no one except Howard."

Nans's gaze darted to the ladies, her eyebrows raised, before continuing her questioning. "Had Mary and Howard been having any difficulties in their relationship that you know of?"

Sylvia scowled. "Well, I really can't talk out of school. Even if I knew something about their relationship, Mary was my friend. Secrets like that demand discretion. Not that I knew anything, mind you. Oh, it's just all so terrible." She dissolved into sobs once more.

"Yes, dear, but Mary's been murdered." Nans waited until Sylvia's tears subsided. "If there was ever a time to divulge something, anything out of the ordinary, it's now."

Sylvia twisted her pearl necklace so tight Lexy feared it might break. "You don't honestly think Howard might have had something to do with Mary's death, do you?" She blinked at them for a moment, her face contorted with grief. Well, as contorted as it could be with an immovable forehead. "No, he couldn't have. I refuse to believe it!" She patted her nose with her tissues. "I mean, he did just buy that new term life insurance policy from Dottie's grandson when he came around selling them here at the center. You ladies remember that, right?"

Nans nodded. "Yes. It was a few weeks ago, right?"

Sylvia nodded. "Yes. Now he would have hardly done that if they didn't get along, would he?"

She exhaled slowly. "I'm not sure about that, dear. *Were* they arguing?"

"No, not that I know of." Sylvia crumpled the tissue in her fist. "I will say that I had been feeling like something wasn't right between them for some time now, as much as it pains me to say. Not any one thing I can put my finger on, just a sense you get when you know two people so well."

Lexy locked eyes with Nans, while Ruth, Helen, and Ida leaned forward in their chairs. Could this be their first clue?

"I understand what you mean, Sylvia dear." Nans patted her hand again, leaning closer to create a sense of intimacy. "Now, you said Mary told you she was going to check with the caterers and put you in charge of handling Chandler Bennington? Is that correct?"

"Yes." Sylvia dabbed her cheeks again. "Mary usually dealt with Bennington, but she passed that task off to me. I wasn't looking forward to it. I'd heard he was obnoxious. Lucky thing I never had to talk to him. The announcement was made, and then there was no reason to."

"What about the trophy for the contest winner?" Lexy asked when Nans paused. "That wasn't originally in the pie room, yet it was found near Mary's body." She left out the part about it being used as the murder weapon, hoping to save them from more hysterics. "Where was that kept?"

"In Mary's office," Sylvia said. "That's what she went back there to get."

"So Mary had it with her then. Makes sense." Nans patted Sylvia's hand again before pushing her chair back. "Well, we don't want to keep you. I'm sure you're busy."

Sylvia gave them a small smile and stood. "Yes, lots to do here even though..." She let her words trail off, her eyes misting again.

Lexy, Ruth, Ida, and Helen all stood.

"Thanks so much for speaking with us, Sylvia. And please let me offer our condolences again on your loss," Nans said as they all started out of the room.

"No problem. Now, if you'll excuse me, I need to check on a few more things in my office." Sylvia headed down the hall, leaving them standing near the closet in the foyer near the front door.

Ida leaned back so she could watch Sylvia. The moment Sylvia walked into her office, Ida turned back to them and whispered, "See? I was right. It's always the husband."

"Not necessarily, Ida. We must not make assumptions." Nans walked slowly toward the front door with Lexy and the ladies beside her. "Let's consider what we *do* know." She stopped just shy of the door and turned to them. "We know that Mary was going back to her office to get the trophy."

"She must have succeeded, because that's what she was killed with," Ida said.

"Why go to the pie room?" Helen asked.

"Maybe to check on something," Lexy suggested.

"Sylvia said she was going to check with the caterers, and she'd gone back to get the trophy." Nans looked at Lexy. "Did she ever check with you?"

Lexy shook her head. "I guess she never made it. Maybe she was looking for me in the pie room when she was killed."

"So the killer skulked down the hallway, saw that she was in the dark pie room alone, and ... *whack!*" Ida made a vigorous clubbing motion.

"Or the killer lured her into the pie room," Ruth suggested.

"Or was already in there, waiting," Nans said. "Maybe the killer was there for another reason and Mary surprised him. Caught him in the act, and he had to kill her."

"The act of what?" Helen asked.

"Messing with the pies." The scowl on Ida's face and the way she said it made pie-messing sound downright felonious.

"I hardly think getting caught messing with pies is reason for murder." Nans glanced back at the hallway. "Interesting thing, though—that hall leads to three places: the kitchen, the pie room, and the offices. Not many people other than Mary, Sylvia, and Lexy would have had a reason to go to any of those rooms. Lexy, did you see anyone in the hallway who shouldn't have been there?"

"The hallway was empty when I went down to check the pie room. Before that, I was fixing the burner under the chafing dish and wasn't looking," Lexy said.

"But Sylvia just said she saw Howard, so I *was* right," Ida said. "He was the only one down there, so he must have killed Mary."

Nans pressed her lips together. "It's something to investigate for sure, but we need to find out more about the timing. It's not unreasonable to think Howard would go down the hall to visit his wife. Sylvia was visibly shaken and might not have remembered correctly when she saw him. We need to find out who else was in that hallway."

Lexy glanced at Helen, who was looking down at her feet.

"Oh no." Ruth's gaze was fixed on the long, narrow window beside the door, where Lexy saw a short, curvy woman with pinkish-blond hair permed into tight little curls. She had to be eighty, and she strutted to the door as if she were heading to the "buy one, get one free" sale at the orthopedic-shoe store.

Ida sighed. "It's Barb Klasky. She's the community busybody. Always running her mouth about someone else's business."

Considering some of the people Lexy had met at the retirement community so far, that meant something. And considering their current situation, she seemed the perfect sort to talk to. Barb whipped open the door and squinted inside, her face lighting up when she saw them.

"Goodness, I'm so glad you're here, Mona," Barb said, charging up to Nans. "I know you and your friends have a reputation for investigating crimes. Are you here snooping for clues today?" She smiled over at Lexy. "And Lexy. How are you?"

"Great," Lexy said.

Barb turned back to Nans. "Tell me what you're up to today, Mona."

"You're right. We are investigating what happened to poor Mary." Nans gave them all a look then nodded. "We've heard that Mary's husband, Howard, might have been involved somehow."

"Oh my! No!" Barb shook her head vigorously. "It couldn't possibly have been Howard."

"Why not?" Ida asked, frowning.

"I saw Howard yesterday, right before the terrible incident, and he had a gift in his hand for her. Now what kind of man would give his wife a gift right before he killed her?" Barb's gaze darted to each of them for effect. "Not a decent man, and poor Howard is nothing if not decent."

Giving an unconvinced-sounding snort, Ida crossed her arms and tapped the toe of her orthopedic shoe on the carpeting. "What kind of a gift was it?"

"I'm not sure, but it was a small box." Barb flashed a sly smile. "In my experience, the best gifts always come in the smallest boxes, if you know what I mean. It was wrapped beautifully too, in pink-flamingo paper with a big frothy bow."

Ruth narrowed her dark gaze. "Are you sure?"

"Yes, positive." Barb straightened. "If you don't believe me, ask Betty Farmer. She was with me when Howard walked by with it, and we both made a comment about how nice it was that a man would continue to buy his wife gifts after forty years of marriage."

Nans exchanged a glance with Lexy at the mention of Betty's name. "Interesting."

"I should say so," Barb said. "So who do you have on your list?"

"Well, I really couldn't say. We don't have anything positive yet. Too early to say for sure. Is there anything else you can remember from last night?

Anything that seemed off or anyone who behaved oddly?" Nans asked.

Barb pressed her lips together and thought for a second. "No, can't say as I do."

"Well, if you think of something, let us know, will you?" Nans headed toward the door in a subtle attempt to let Barb know the conversation was over. Barb was the type that would talk all day if you let her.

"Will do!" Barb called after them as they headed into the parking lot.

Lexy fished in her bag for the key, glancing over at Ruth, who was staring at Helen. Helen had remained unusually quiet since they'd arrived at the center. Something was definitely up. Lexy just hadn't had time to figure out exactly what. She wasn't sure what to make of it. Surely if Helen had seen something pertaining to the murder, she wouldn't hide it from them.

"What's wrong with you?" Ruth finally asked Helen with her usual bluntness. "Not feeling well?"

"Poor thing is probably starved for carbs," Ida said. "Maybe you need to break down and have a doughnut or something. Get back to a regular diet again."

Helen gave a dismissive wave and mumbled something under her breath before turning away. Lexy couldn't help wondering if her pensive mood had more to do with her being in the hallway just before Mary was killed than with low blood sugar. Had she seen something? Was she afraid to tell them?

Lexy finally dug out her car fob and pressed the unlock button. The car chirped, and Nans grabbed the passenger-side door.

"When do you pick up Sprinkles?" Nans asked.

Lexy looked at her watch. "Not for another hour."

"Hmm ... so we can verify with her about the gift then. In the meanwhile, there's one thing we need to do."

"What's that?" Ruth asked.

"Why, go to Lexy's bakery, of course. We can chow down on a few pastries, Helen can improve her disposition, and then we can pack a nice box of goodies to take along with our condolences to the grieving widower."

CHAPTER SIX

$\mathcal{N}$ans and the ladies picked out an assortment of pastries for Howard and, of course, some for themselves. Helen, though, stuck to her low-carb intentions, pulling a piece of string cheese from her purse and meticulously pulling strings off and eating them while the others shoved cupcakes into their faces.

Twenty minutes later, they pulled to the curb in front of Howard and Mary Archer's house. The small ranch-style home had a well-kept yard. No other cars were parked in the driveway or on the street. That meant they'd be the only condolence wishers around. Talking to Howard about his wife's death was probably best done without other mourners listening in.

Lexy felt a pang of guilt. Should they really be

questioning the man the day after his wife was murdered? It seemed a bit insensitive. Then again, wishing him condolences could be comforting. Forty years of marriage. Lexy couldn't imagine losing Jack now, let alone after all that time. It would be devastating.

Two rocking chairs sat on one side of the porch, with a table between them, upon which was a pot of wilting pansies. Nans knocked on the door, and Howard answered on the second round. The poor man looked decidedly disheveled, in his wrinkled shirt and pants topped with a threadbare bathrobe, his stockinged feet sticking out from beneath the hem of his trousers. Dark circles rimmed his eyes behind his glasses, and his dark-gray hair stuck up at odd angles. His expression was a blend of annoyance and deep sorrow. He didn't look like a man who'd just killed his wife. He looked like a man who'd lost his best friend, his life partner, his everything. But maybe he was a good actor.

"Howard," Nans said, holding out the box of pastries. "We wanted to stop by and offer our condolences on Mary's passing. We're so very sorry for your loss."

"Oh." He stared down at the white box tied with pink-and-white bakery twine then back up at each of them. The irritation and darkness left his expression, replaced by appreciation. "Thank you. Please, won't you come in?"

Inside, the place looked like what you'd expect for a man who'd been married for four decades and suddenly found himself alone. Even though it hadn't even been twenty-four hours, mail and assorted newspapers were scattered about the tables and sofa. Plates of half-eaten food joined the mix, probably left over from Mary's cooking or perhaps goodwill offerings brought by neighbors. He hurried to clear spaces for them to sit.

Lexy couldn't help feeling sorry for the man despite what he might have done. He seemed truly discombobulated, so she stepped in to help. "Howard, I'm Nans's granddaughter, Lexy. We've met in passing at the community center, but I'm not sure you remember me. Anyway, why don't you sit down and relax, and I'll make us some fresh coffee to enjoy with these pastries. Does that sound all right?"

His shoulders sagged with relief. "Yes, please. That sounds lovely. Mary always played hostess. I'm afraid I'm not very good at it. No idea what I'm doing."

Lexy gave him a small smile and made her way to the kitchen, picking up the dirty plates and glasses along the way. Ruth, Ida, and Helen joined Nans on the sofa to sit with Howard and make small talk while Lexy fumbled around in the tiny 1970s avocado-and-gold kitchen, putting things away then setting the scones out on a plate. She went in search of the makings for coffee. She found the coffee and filters in the third cabinet and set up the coffee machine with a new filter for the job.

Mary and Howard kept the trash under the sink. As she tossed the package from the filters, something bright pink caught her eye. She pulled the trash out, sadness washing over her when she saw scraps of pink-flamingo wrapping paper. Just as Barb had said, Howard had wrapped a gift for his wife, and judging by the cut-up pieces, he wasn't a very good wrapper. It reminded Lexy of the excess paper Jack had to cut off of the gifts he wrapped for her. But would Howard take the time to wrap a gift for his wife before killing her? Had they gotten into a fight? Maybe Mary didn't like the gift.

Lexy waited for the coffee to perk then carried the whole tray into the living room, where she found Nans and the ladies making small talk with Howard. She poured coffee for everyone, and they all picked a pastry from the dish while Nans got down to some gentle interrogation.

"Howard, what happened to Mary was truly

despicable." She nibbled on her ham-and-cheese scone. "But I have to ask—do you know anyone who would want to hurt her?"

"No, no." Howard frowned down into his cup, his fingers trembling slightly. "Absolutely not. That's just the thing. Everyone loved her."

"Hmm." Ruth sipped her coffee, watching Howard over the rim of her cup. "Perhaps the murder wasn't about her, then. Maybe it was about something she had in her possession. Can you think of anything she might have owned that someone else would desperately want? The contest trophy? Or what about the signed book?"

Howard scrunched his nose. "That trophy wasn't worth more than twenty dollars. I picked it up at the shop the other day. And that book came from a garage sale. Who'd want to kill for either of those things?"

"Well, I find it terribly sad." Nans sighed, setting her cup on the table. "Especially after you'd just given her that lovely gift."

"What?" Howard shifted in his seat, his gaze lowered and his expression uncomfortable. "I don't know anything about a gift."

"Really?" Ida piped in around a mouthful of scone. "You didn't give her a gift right before she died? I thought I heard you mention that."

Nans gave Ida a stern look before continuing. "Either way, how awful you must feel knowing that you could have prevented her murder."

"I don't know what you mean," Howard said, scowling. "I had no idea that was going to happen. How in the world could I have possibly prevented it?"

"Well, you were there outside her office just moments before she left to go to the pie room, weren't you?" Nans blinked at him innocently. "That's what Sylvia Hensel told us. Perhaps if you'd just kept your beloved wife there a few moments longer, the killer might not have had the opportunity to attack her."

Face red, Howard leaned forward, his eyes glittering with anger behind his glasses. "Now you listen to me, Mona. I don't know where you ladies are getting your information, but it had better be from a more reliable source than Sylvia Hensel. I was nowhere near Mary's office either before or after she died. You can take that to the bank."

"Oh, goodness." Nans's tone turned apologetic, dripping with faux remorse. "Well, we certainly never meant to imply that you had anything to do with what happened to your Mary, Howard. I'm so sorry. We were just trying to put all the pieces together." Then she smiled, one Lexy had seen many times on her grandmother's face right before she went in for a direct strike. "But if you don't mind me asking, and all in the spirit of having a well-rounded picture of things, where exactly *were* you when Mary was killed? If you weren't outside her office, that is."

"Playing poker." Howard gestured across the sofa to Ruth. "She was there. Don't you remember? I was in the poker room the whole time. She saw me."

Ruth winced under everyone's direct scrutiny then nodded. "He was. I forgot."

"Right." Howard pushed to his feet and headed for the front door, holding it open as he gestured back. "I think it's about time for you ladies to leave."

Ida quickly shoved the last of her scone into her mouth then grabbed a second from the box and dropped it into her purse before following the rest of the ladies back out onto the porch.

"Are you sure you wouldn't like us to stay a bit longer?" Lexy asked at the threshold, unable to get the picture of that wrapping paper out of her mind. He'd had the gift, just as Barb had said, but he was lying about it. Maybe if they could talk to him longer, they'd find out why. Even though Lexy had to pick Sprinkles up from the groomer, she could be a few minutes late. She still had a feeling that Howard was not the killer. Maybe he'd simply forgotten or blocked it from his memory as too painful. "I could help tidy up a bit and warm you something for dinner later on."

"No, thank you. I believe you ladies have done quite enough. Good day!" With that, Howard closed the door in their faces.

They slunk back to the VW, Nans and the others chatting about what they'd just learned.

"Well, that was a complete bust," Helen said.

"Did you really see Howard at that poker game?" Nans asked.

"Now that I think about it, I did." Ruth shrugged. "Sorry I got that wrong earlier. It was just so chaotic. There were multiple tables, and the room was busy, but I do remember seeing him in there. And he was there for a while."

Lexy walked around to the driver's side of the car and clicked the fob to unlock the doors. "Well, there is one thing he is lying about for certain. I saw the flamingo wrapping paper that Barb said the gift was wrapped with in the trash in the kitchen."

"Interesting," Nans said, holding the seat forward so Ruth, Helen, and Ida could get into the back. "But Howard said he'd never given Mary a gift. Which means he lied. Why would he do that?"

Ida chuckled. "Maybe his gift wasn't for his wife."

Once they were all settled in the vehicle, Lexy

started the engine and pulled out onto the quiet residential street while the ladies continued to discuss the case.

"There could be other reasons Howard lied about that gift," Helen said.

"Like what?" Nans asked, catching her eye in the rearview mirror.

"Maybe Barb was mistaken in what she saw," Ruth offered. "Lord knows she does like to exaggerate."

"True," Ida said, stuffing half of her second scone in her mouth. Lexy made a mental note to vacuum the car later to pick up all those loose crumbs.

Nans looked at her watch. "Good thing we have perfect timing, then. It's just about time for Lexy to pick up Sprinkles. We can verify with Betty Farmer if there really was a gift."

he Pampered Pooch was just outside the center of town. A 1960s split-level converted into a business, it was painted a crisp white with red shutters and decked out with flower boxes under the windows.

Lexy and the ladies headed inside, where the smell of dog shampoo and the barking of pampered pets permeated the air. They waited while Betty rang up another customer before approaching the desk.

It was a nice business, with a small doggy boutique in the front set in the large bay window of the former living room. The boutique sold clothes and accessories and all types of gear for canine friends. They'd taken out the top half of the wall that once separated the living room from the kitchen and installed a glass window that looked into the grooming area.

Three groomers were working. One had a large black lab on her table, and the other two were working on what looked to be Pomeranians, given their fluffy, puffball hairstyles and superior small-canine attitudes. Betty was dressed in pink scrubs adorned with all different kinds of doggy faces, the same as the rest of her staff.

"Hi, Lexy! Sprinkles did great today. She's relaxing in one of the spa rooms. I'll go get her." Betty went down the hallway to the closed rooms that were once bedrooms and were now converted into plush kennels. A few seconds later, she emerged with Sprinkles, all spiffed up with a sparkly pink bow and painted pink nails.

Sprinkles started fidgeting and wiggling as soon as she spotted Lexy. Betty placed her in Lexy's arms, and the fruity smell of shampoo wafted up as Lexy dodged a barrage of wet, slobbering doggy kisses.

"She looks great," Lexy said, shifting Sprinkles onto her hip so she could reach into her purse to pay Betty, who had slipped behind the cash register again.

"This is a great place you have here," Nans said. "Kind of like a hair salon but for pets."

"That's exactly what it is!" Betty beamed as she glanced around her shop proudly.

"I bet you get good gossip here too. Just like in a hair salon," Ida said.

You had to hand it to the ladies; they knew how to get the conversation rolling toward exactly what they wanted to discuss.

"That we do." Betty handed the credit card back to Lexy.

"So you probably heard some scuttlebutt about Mary Archer." Nans tried to act nonchalant.

Betty glanced around the shop and lowered her voice even though no one else was present. "It's just terrible. Mary was such a nice person. Can't imagine why anyone would want to do her in." Betty sighed. "And poor Howard. He must be heartsick about all this."

"We just came from his house, actually," Lexy said. "We wanted to check in and make sure he was all right." Sprinkles squirmed in her arms to get down, so she slipped her into her harness, clipped her leash, and set her on the floor while she finished signing the credit card slip. "Hard to believe they were married forty years. Rumor has it he was going to give Mary a gift right before she died."

Lexy looked at Nans from beneath her lashes,

catching a quick smile from her grandmother at how she'd deftly worked in the one question they'd really wanted to ask.

"Oh yes!" Betty said, shaking her head. "I'd forgotten about that, but I saw it. Pretty little package. With that pink paper and bows. Too bad it was probably to make up for the argument."

"Argument?" Nans stepped forward at last, her face alight with interest. "Howard and Mary had an argument?"

"No. The fight was between Mary and that awful Chandler Bennington character. I bet poor Howard just wanted to make Mary feel better afterward. He's such a kind, thoughtful man, that Howard."

"Huh." Nans narrowed her gaze. "Did you see this argument between Mary and Chandler? Was it heated? Did things turn violent?"

"Yeah, I'd say it was heated," Betty said, leaning her elbows on the counter. "But not violent. I try not to eavesdrop, mind you, but from what I overheard, it was something about that book she was giving away for the pie-eating contest. He wanted her to reconsider."

"Reconsider what?" Nans asked, frowning. "Giving the book away as a prize?"

"I'm not sure." Betty shrugged. "Like I said, I'm no spy. But I don't think he ever said, now that I think about it. But maybe he just wanted it back or something."

"That doesn't make any sense," Ruth said from behind Nans. "If the author didn't want her giving away that old book, then why would he come all the way here to present it to the winner himself?"

"Again, no idea." Betty gave a one-shoulder shrug. "All I can tell you for certain is that he said he wanted to look at the book, and Mary said there wasn't time. She told him he should've asked her earlier, and that's when he got all put out and yelled at her about how he tried many times and that the organizers of the event were not being very accommodating to his wishes."

"What happened after that?" Helen asked. "Where did they go after the argument?"

"Your guess is as good as mine. I walked away at that point." Betty looked sheepish. "I'd been standing behind one of those tall balloon arrangements in the corner, and I didn't want to get caught."

Sprinkles started to do a little jig by the door, and Lexy suspected she had some urgent business. "Well, thank you for grooming Sprinkles, Betty. I'll see you next month."

"See you then." Betty waved before returning to the back of her shop.

Lexy and the ladies headed back out to the VW,

stopping along the way so Sprinkles could do her business. Once they were all back in the car, Nans tried to hold Sprinkles on her lap in the passenger seat, but the dog was having none of it. She was far more interested in climbing into the back. Nans pulled her back to her lap, but Sprinkles tried to slip between the front seats. Nans pulled back, and Sprinkles tried again.

"Oh, just let her come back here. I'll hold her." Ida held her hands out, and Nans let go.

Sprinkles leaped into Ida's lap but didn't stop there. She crawled across Ida, then Ruth, and went right to Helen and got busy sniffing Helen's giant purse.

Satisfied that Sprinkles was secure with the ladies in back, Lexy started the car and headed toward the retirement center. "So, what about this new information on Chandler Bennington?"

Ruth sniffed. "Sounds to me like he thought it was too generous to give his book as a prize in a pie-eating contest and he wanted it back."

"Pfft." Ida scoffed. "How much can that ratty old book be worth anyway? That guy isn't even that famous. He writes about a pie-baking detective, for goodness' sake." She scowled. "Wasn't even like that book was such a great prize to begin with. I'd much rather have had two tickets to the early-bird special at Cactus Joe's."

"I told Mary that myself, but she said we didn't have enough money in the coffers for gift certificates to a restaurant," Ruth said. "She was quite pleased she'd saved the community center so much money by getting that book at a yard sale for a quarter. You know we don't have a lot of discretionary funds. That's why we had to let go of the on-site security and issue key cards."

"Betty did say that Chandler was angry," Nans said. "And anger makes for a good motive. But *why* would he be angry? That's the thing I don't understand. I mean, I suppose it could just be his personality to be disagreeable. Everyone seems to describe him as eccentric and moody and generally unfit for human companionship."

"And the guy writes about murder—don't forget," Ida added. "Isn't such a jump for him to go from writing about it to actually doing it, eh? Not to mention that the guy didn't eat any pie! That right there's suspicious, if you ask me."

"He kept his hands in his pockets the whole time too," Ruth said. "I noticed every time I saw him that they were tucked away inside his pockets. Now I wonder if he wasn't trying to hide something, like maybe scratches or pie under his nails from what he did to poor Mary."

"Pie?" Nans asked, frowning.

"Yes, pie." Ruth gave her a flat look. "Mary was found facedown in a pie. I'd assume whoever killed her got it on his hands. And Lexy said Jack and the police confiscated those pies as evidence because it looked as though someone had been digging around in them, right? There were blueberry pies and strawberry. Both of those stain."

"Yes!" Ida exclaimed, making everyone jump. "Pie stains! Blueberry pie stains something awful, and that's the kind of pie Mary was facedown in. The filling was all over the tablecloth and floor in the pie room. I bet that's it. That's why he had to hide his hands. Why, the last time I ate some at the bakery, I had to clean my dentures three times to remove the stains."

Helen didn't say a word, just sitting in her corner of the back seat, trying to shoo Sprinkles away from her handbag.

Nans had apparently had enough of her silent behavior because she turned around to give Helen a look over her shoulder. "Helen, what do you think?"

Helen snatched her purse away from Sprinkles and looked up at Nans. "Well, it could have been Chandler, but it's usually someone close to the victim."

Nans studied Helen for a while. "That's it? You need to eat some carbs, my friend. You're turning into a real Debbie Downer with this new diet of yours."

Lexy kept driving, unable to keep from wondering if there was more to Helen's change in attitude than her diet. Her mind drifted to an image of Helen in the hallway right before Mary was killed.

"Chandler Bennington is staying at the Wayfarer Motel out on Route 6," Ruth said as they pulled into the parking lot in front of the community center. "I overheard Mary mention it the other day."

"What are we waiting for, then?" Ida asked. "Let's go see him. The diner next door to the motel has great BLTs."

Lexy glanced back at Sprinkles. "Well, I guess I can drop Sprinkles off and ask Cassie to hold down the fort at the bakery."

"Great!" Nans clapped her hands. "We can talk to Chandler and get him to confess to Mary's murder then celebrate with a late lunch at the diner."

CHAPTER EIGHT

he Wayfarer Hotel was not exactly the Ritz Carlton. Built in the midsixties, it had the same sort of exterior as an old Howard Johnson, minus the neon-orange-and-blue paint. It wasn't rundown, necessarily, but Lexy was sure it wasn't up to Chandler Bennington's lofty standards. Still, it was about the best in their tiny town.

Thankfully, Ruth knew the lady at the desk, Sophie Collins, from bingo, and she eagerly gave them Chandler's room number. She made a face when they asked, as if she'd had about enough of their esteemed guest. Once again, Lexy was reminded of the rumors of Chandler being eccentric and hard to get along with. But that didn't necessarily mean he was a killer.

They left the air-conditioned office and traipsed

down the row of doors, Ida fanning herself in the heat. It was going to be another scorcher, and Lexy was glad she'd worn a thin T-shirt and linen capris.

They knocked on Chandler's door three times before he answered. He was as rude as everyone had said.

"What do you want?" he asked, glaring at them. "You people need to leave me alone."

Nans, seemingly undeterred by his nastiness, craned her neck to look over his shoulder into his room. Lexy did the same. Inside was about what she'd expected: dark-brown paneled walls, orange-and-gold floral bedspread, and avocado-green shag rug. A suitcase sat open on the bed.

"Going somewhere?" Nans asked. "Looks like you're packing. Don't tell me you're skipping town, Mr. Bennington."

"Not that it's any of your business," he said, "but I'm leaving tomorrow. My flight was prearranged before I ever came here. You can check. And I can't say I'll be sorry to say goodbye to this two-bit town."

"Hmm," Ruth said. "So, the police are allowing you to leave?"

"Of course." He gave her an annoyed stare. "Why wouldn't they? I'm under no suspicion."

Nans and Lexy exchanged a we'll-see-about-that look.

Nans got right down to business. "We happen to have a witness who saw you arguing with Mary Archer shortly before she was murdered."

"That's ridiculous," Chandler said. "I never argued with Mary Archer. Despite how rude she was. In fact"—he gave them all a disparaging look—"everyone I've met in Brook Ridge is incredibly rude. Especially that drill sergeant in pearls, as I like to call her. Stephanie Hazlett or whatever her name is. All brown bob and broomsticks, she is. That one isn't accommodating at all. I can't even remember her name now. Do you know who I'm talking about?"

"I believe you're referring to our friend, Sylvia Hensel," Nans said by way of answer to his question but chose instead to focus on the book instead of his insults. "Why were you interested in getting your old novel back, Mr. Bennington?"

"What?" He wrinkled his nose.

"The book Mary Archer had as a prize for the contest. The one you came here to present to the winner. Our witness said she overheard you arguing with Mary about it. Why were you trying to take it back?"

"Again, not that it's any of your concern, but I wasn't trying to take that blasted book back. All I wanted to do was *look* at it." He sighed. "To verify my signature. But she wouldn't even let me do that. Lord, you would've thought they were giving away the Dead Sea Scrolls, as tightly as they kept that silly old book locked up."

He'd been standing halfway behind the door the whole time they were talking, with Lexy and the ladies still out on the sidewalk. Unfortunately, given their positions, his hands weren't visible.

"Sorry, Mr. Bennington," Nans said, "but I'm not buying your story. Something strange is going on, and we're going to get to the bottom of it." Nans squared her shoulders and lifted her chin defiantly. "I want to know exactly where you were at the time Mary Archer was killed."

"Who died and made you chief of police?" he challenged.

They all advanced a step toward him, and Chandler Bennington's eyes widened, his pugnacious expression faltering. He cleared his throat and shuffled his feet. "Fine. I had nothing to do with her death. I swear. No guilt here." He looked away. "I don't even know when she died, so how can I tell you where I was?" His eyes narrowed. "Wait, was that some kind of trick question? I think I might have used that one in a book once."

"No," Nans said. "We don't resort to tricks. Mary died shortly before Lexy announced the pie-eating contest was canceled. Where were you just before you heard the announcement?"

Lexy had secured the hallway for the police right after she'd found Mary's body and as she announced the contest was canceled. Mary had not been dead long, so the killer would have been in the pie room shortly before that. If Chandler didn't have anyone who could vouch for his whereabouts, he could very well be the killer.

Lexy glanced into the hotel room again. If he'd killed once, he might kill again. It was a lucky thing they'd all come together. There was no way he could overpower all of them and drag them into his room to silence them.

"Fine. If you must know, I was at the bar, sipping a scotch. I got there a short time before all the commotion started down the hall. Then the announcement was made, and I continued sitting there until the police arrived." He looked at Lexy. "You should know that. You passed right by me on your way to the buffet."

Lexy thought back. She had seen him at the bar,

but that was before she noticed the burner was out under the chafing dish for the scalloped potatoes and she'd detoured to light it before proceeding to the pie room. How long had Mary been dead? Could Chandler have had time to get up from the bar, race down to the room, and kill Mary in the time Lexy was lighting the burners under the chafing dishes? "Yes, but that was quite a bit before the body was discovered."

"Well, between you and the other one, surely you can figure out that I was at the bar the whole time." Chandler huffed.

Nans frowned. "Other one? What other one?"

Chandler looked at Nans as if she were daft then jerked his chin toward Helen. "That one right there. She was hovering in the hallway next to the bar with a dazed look on her face. Then, suddenly, she darted past the bar, practically knocking me over. A few minutes later, the announcement was made."

They all turned to stare at Helen, who shuffled her feet, her eyes wide. She didn't say a word.

"That's right," Chandler continued, on a roll now. "She practically ran me over on her way past the bar while I was simply trying to get to my stool after ordering my drink. No apology or anything. She just barreled on through with this crazed look in her eyes, holding onto that purse of hers for dear life. So I stayed put. Felt safer that way. Nursed my drink and watched the festivities fall apart once the announcement came that the contest was called off due to murder. Ghastly, really. Worst of all, I'd barely gotten two sips of my drink down before the cops pulled me away for questioning."

CHAPTER NINE

"So, you were in the hallway then?" Nans asked Helen as they sat around an old-fashioned chrome-and-Formica table in the diner, munching on BLTs. Ida had been right. The things were pretty amazing. Crisp lettuce, ripe and juicy tomatoes, and salty bacon slathered with just the right amount of mayo, stacked high on perfectly toasted homemade white bread.

Lexy took a swallow of iced tea and waited, the red Naugahyde booth seat squeaking as she shifted position. She still hadn't mentioned to anyone that she'd seen Helen in the hallway near the entrance right before she'd found Mary Archer's body in the pie room. Helen clutched her handbag to her chest like a shield, and Lexy still couldn't figure out why'd she'd lied about being there. Well, she hadn't really lied, not exactly; she'd just not mentioned that little detail whenever the opportunity came up.

Helen buckled under the pressure. "Fine. Yes. I was there, in the hallway."

"But why?" Ruth asked around a bite of sandwich. "What were you doing?"

"And why didn't you say so before?" Ida lifted the top slice of her sandwich bread and redistributed the bacon more evenly then put the bread back on and patted it for good measure before picking up the sandwich and chomping off the corner.

Helen's cheeks flushed as she stared down at her lap. "I was in the kitchen, sneaking piecrust, okay?" To prove her point, she opened that precious purse of hers to show them the interior. Crumbs and hunks of crust clung to the expensive silk lining. "See? And don't worry, Lexy. I only took it from the pies your assistant had deemed not pretty enough to use in the contest. At least I think so. I didn't go into the pie room."

Lexy's shoulders relaxed. "Well, at least that explains why Sprinkles was so interested in your purse."

"Why would you lie about that, though?" Nans asked.

"I didn't want anyone to know I was cheating on

my diet." Helen sighed. "Rena doesn't treat carb cheaters kindly."

Ida scoffed. "Carbs, schmarbs. What I want to know is if you saw anything while you were stuffing your face with crust in the hall. You were there around the time Mary's killer struck. Surely you must've seen something. They had to get into and out of that pie room from the hallway. It's the only access."

"I wish I had, but no." Helen shrugged. "I was so busy making sure no one saw me come from the forbidden kitchen area that I didn't pay much attention to anything else. But I can corroborate that Sylvia and Mary were in the office, as Sylvia told us earlier. I heard them talking. But again, with all the other noise and my sneaking around, I wasn't really able to hear what they said."

"How about Howard?" Nans pushed her empty plate away. "You must have run into him on your way out. He would've been in the hallway about the same time as you. Sylvia said she saw him."

"No, I didn't see him. Honestly, I didn't see anyone. I rushed straight from the kitchen with my haul, stopped briefly near the bar to get my bearings, then headed straight for the bathroom. I figured I could hide in one of the stalls and eat my piecrust in peace." Helen shook her head. "No such luck. As soon as I got in there, Vera Masterson and Anne O'Neil walked in, and I got stuck listening to them complain."

"What were they complaining about?" Ida asked while sneaking a few fries from Ruth's plate.

"Chandler Bennington, mostly. They mentioned he'd been rude to Lorelei Summers." Helen sniffed. "Apparently, she'd asked him to sign some of his books she'd purchased for her antiques store, and he refused. Doesn't surprise me, considering how rude the man is to everyone."

"Well, this doesn't make sense," Lexy said, frowning. "If Chandler didn't see anyone, and Helen didn't see anyone, and Sylvia only saw Howard, how did the killer get in and out?"

"Maybe he was already down there, lurking," Ruth said, raising a brow.

"Hmm. But that couldn't have worked either," Nans said. "The offices are down at the end. If he was already in there, someone should've seen him come out. Sylvia only saw Howard heading toward Mary's office, not coming out again."

"There's another possibility," Ida said, devouring another bite of her sandwich. "Maybe Chandler's lying, and he went into the pie room and killed Mary as soon as Helen went into the bathroom. He and

Howard are about the same build, right? Maybe Sylvia saw Chandler, not Howard."

Nans sat back and crossed her arms. "If that's the case, then it all comes back to that book of his that Mary had. Because as far as I know, he didn't know Mary before this. He would have no motive to kill her. Speaking of which..." Nans sat forward, looking around at each of us. "Whatever happened to the book prize for the pie-eating contest?" She narrowed her gaze on Lexy. "Did Jack mention the book being near Mary's body in the pie room? Did the police take it?"

"No. He didn't mention anything last night." Lexy finished her tea. "And the only thing I saw near the body was the trophy the killer used to bash her head in. And all that blueberry filling."

"Hmm," Nans said and stood.

Everyone followed, throwing money down on the table. Ida pulled a napkin out of the stainless-steel dispenser on the table and wrapped the rest of her sandwich before shoving it in her purse.

Nans continued, "Perhaps we have been on the wrong trail. Let's head back to my apartment. We'll reevaluate our clues and go from there, ladies. I'm starting to believe the motive might be different from what we originally suspected."

CHAPTER TEN

*O*nce they were all back in her apartment, Nans wheeled out her whiteboard again. Ruth put on coffee, Helen set the table, and Ida pulled the napkin-wrapped sandwich from her purse. Lexy got busy taking some pastries out of Nans's fridge, and soon, they were all seated around the table with refreshments in hand.

Nans took her place at the whiteboard, opened her stinky red marker, and pointed toward the lists. "Right, so here's what we know so far: the husband, Howard, seems to have an alibi. He was at the poker game, and there're plenty of witnesses to corroborate, including you, Ruth."

Ruth nodded, her mouth full of day-old Danish.

"Though I suppose we should nail down the

timing on that. And maybe ask some of the others," Nans continued.

Ruth nodded again.

"So, it couldn't have been him. Unless he was in it with someone else and they did the dirty work," Helen said.

"Sylvia made it sound as though they weren't getting along and he was nervous about the gift. Maybe Ida's right and it was for someone else," Lexy suggested.

Ida snorted. "I usually am. If he was having an affair, that would give him motive to get rid of her."

"I don't know," Helen said. "Howard sure did seem upset earlier."

"Maybe he didn't really want to kill her but had some gambling debts he had to pay off." Ida turned to Ruth. "How was he acting in the poker game? Desperate?"

Ruth thought for a second. "I wouldn't say he was desperate. He was acting the same as the rest of us. Though now that you mention it, he might have been a little nervous. He flubbed a few hands."

Nans added that information to the board and then moved to the side again so they could all see. "What else?"

"Sylvia mentioned a new life insurance policy he bought from Dottie's grandson," Ruth said.

"Hmm..." Ida finished her sandwich and reached for a brownie. "I was thinking if he owed some thugs, he might have taken out a big insurance policy on Mary and had to do her in to collect. I mean, if thugs are going to break your arms or make you sleep with the fishes, you might kill your spouse even if you don't want to."

Lexy glanced at Nans. "That seems a little far-fetched. Don't you think?"

Nans shrugged. "We should consider every possibility." She scribbled on the whiteboard and then looked back at them over her shoulder. "We should have a talk with Dottie because her grandson sold Howard that policy. See what she knows."

Ida snorted. "If it was a huge amount, then I say we need to look into Howard further."

"Agreed." Nans narrowed her gaze at the whiteboard. "Then there is Chandler Bennington. Why was he so sneaky at the party, and why did he demand to see the book from Mary? He said it was to check the signature, but Mary said he'd signed it decades ago. What was he checking for? Did he think it was a fake?"

"Why would someone forge his signature?" Ida

asked. "Darn book wasn't worth very much, near as I could tell."

"There's one way to find out." Helen pulled her tablet computer from her purse, brushed off pie crumbs, and set it on the table. She typed on the screen then hit the return key.

"Oh my," Helen said.

"What?" Nans looked over her shoulder. "Is that a joke?"

"What is it?" Ruth grabbed the iPad and slid it to face her and Lexy.

Lexy did a double take. The screen showed an eBay auction for *The Catcher in the Pie* with a high bid of ten thousand dollars.

"Ten thousand? Really?" Ruth's eyes were glued to the screen.

"But how could someone list the book from our contest so quickly?" Lexy asked. "Wouldn't they be afraid of getting caught?"

"I don't think this was the book from our contest." Helen slid the iPad back in front of her and squinted at the screen. "It couldn't be. This auction was held a few weeks ago."

"Huh." Ida frowned. "I suppose someone else could have seen this on the Internet and put two and two together. What if they killed Mary because they thought our book was worth just as much?"

"But Mary didn't think it was worth anything," Ruth pointed out. "She told me that just last week. And no one else would've had access to it because she kept it locked in the safe in her office."

Nans made more notes on the whiteboard. "Yes, it doesn't seem too many people disagreed with her about the book being worthless, at least from what they've told us. I mean, who would think that ratty old book she bought for a quarter would bring in a small fortune? Everyone we've talked to thought it was a crappy prize."

"But in today's world, ten grand is hardly worth killing for," Ida said.

"Maybe the killer was only trying to steal the book," Lexy suggested. "What if Mary caught the killer snooping around in her office and things turned ugly?"

"But she was killed in the pie room, not her office. She would have had to follow the killer there, or he or she followed her. And again, who would want to do that? Who would have any idea of the book's true value?" Nans turned to stare at the board again. "So far, the only two I see are Chandler Bennington and maybe Lorelei Summers. She's an antiques dealer and would know the price of collectibles."

"And Lorelei did want him to sign more," Helen added. "At least that's what I heard Vera and Anne gossiping about in the bathroom."

"She might want more signed books if she knew they were worth ten grand. It also makes sense that Chandler would know the value of his own books, right?" Nans asked.

Ida nodded. "And he argued with Mary over getting a peek at it. Maybe the value was in the signature and he wanted to verify it was indeed his before he stole it or demanded she give it back."

"So, the murder was about the book the whole time, then," Ida said, sitting forward. "Not getting rid of poor Mary. She was just caught in the crossfire."

"But what about the problems between Howard and Mary, and the gift?" Ruth asked.

"Oh, Howard still could have been fooling around," Lexy said, remembering the wrapping paper she'd found in his trash. "But that doesn't mean he killed his wife. Lots of men have affairs but never murder anyone."

"Let's not forget that right now, Howard has an alibi," Nans said.

"Chandler does too." Lexy rubbed her eyes and

stifled a yawn. "This doesn't seem to be getting us anywhere."

"But *does* he have an alibi?" Helen glanced at Lexy. "I saw him at the bar, the same as you, Lexy, but he could have just as easily slipped down the hall after I turned to head to the bathroom and you were busy at the buffet table. In that short time, he could have killed Mary. And I can't help wondering why he continues to hide his hands. He did so at the party and at the hotel too. If they did have blueberry stains all over them, then he sure wouldn't want anyone to see them."

"But it's basically our word against his regarding his location." Nans scowled at the whiteboard now covered in suppositions. "He swears he was at the bar at the time Mary was killed. And we all know those security cameras in the community center are just for show. No tape in them."

"He could have lied," Ida said. "Can we talk to the bartender?"

"I think he was a private contractor, like me," Lexy said, "but I'll see if I can track down his info and confirm Chandler's whereabouts. Or I can check with Jack to see if he's done the same already."

"Yes, do that." Nans had a cat-that-ate-the-canary smile on her face. "And while you're at it, mention the book. I bet the police haven't stumbled onto that yet."

Ida nodded. "Yeah, but don't rub his nose in it. We don't want them to realize that we have to do their jobs for them all the time. They might stop cooperating with us."

"Yes, inform him gently," Helen said. "So what do we do next?"

"Until we can place Chandler in the hallway, there's nothing more to be done there. I say our next move is to nail down the timing of it all." Nans glanced at the clock on her wall, which read five thirty. "Lexy, tonight, you find out what the police have gleaned. See if they talked to the bartender and if Chandler or anyone else really does have a solid alibi. Tomorrow, we'll go back to the community center and find out about this book. If it's not there, we may have just discovered the real motive for Mary's death."

CHAPTER ELEVEN

*a*fter leaving Nans's apartment, Lexy checked in with Cassie at the bakery and helped her close up shop before heading home to dinner with Jack. She was eager to compare notes about the case with him, especially after the ladies had uncovered a few clues that the police might not have stumbled upon.

As usual, Sprinkles greeted her at the door with exuberant energy. Her newly polished pink nails clicked on the hardwood floor as she danced at Lexy's feet. Lexy scooped her up, suffered through a barrage of slobbery dog kisses, and carried her into the kitchen, where Jack was elbow deep in marinara sauce. The air smelled of garlic and baking cheese, and despite the BLT earlier, Lexy's stomach growled. She put Sprinkles down and wrapped her arms around Jack's waist from behind. "Hey, baby. I'm home."

He gave her a quick kiss over his shoulder then went back to stirring his pot of sauce. "How'd the investigation go today? Did Nans and the ladies uncover anything useful?"

"It went pretty well." It was so nice, the two of them working together on a case instead of Jack always admonishing her about investigating with Nans or telling her to stay out of it. Still, she didn't want him to think the ladies had gotten carried away and were taking over for the police, so she held back a bit on the enthusiasm. She picked a lettuce leaf out of the salad bowl and nibbled nonchalantly as she continued her answer. "We went to the retirement center and talked to a couple people and then asked Betty a couple of questions when I went to pick up Sprinkles because she was at the party too. Oh, and we went to the hotel to talk to Chandler Bennington."

"Wow, you did have a busy day." The timer went off, and he picked up the pot of boiling pasta and dumped it into a colander in the sink. Steam rose between them. "So, what did Bennington have to say for himself?"

"He acted a little suspicious." Lexy opened drawers and cabinets as she spoke, gathering plates and flatware to set the table. "He was very cagey when Nans asked him about his books. And he kept hiding his hands. I wanted to see if they had blueberry stains from the pies. I remembered you said you thought the killer was looking for something in them."

"Good thinking, honey." Jack returned the drained pasta to the pot before adding the homemade sauce. "What else did you hear?"

"Let's see. It turns out Helen was cheating on her low-carb diet by sneaking piecrusts to eat because she didn't want the woman who's in charge of their fitness plan to find out. She ended up hiding in a bathroom stall to eat them. But it turns out that helped us, because that's where she overheard a conversation between Vera Masterson and Anne O'Neil about a fight Lorelei Summers had with Chandler Bennington."

"Lord save me from women and their diets." Jack rolled his eyes and grinned as he took the garlic bread from the oven. "What did Lorelei and Chandler fight about?"

"Gossip had it that she wanted him to sign some of his books that she had in her antiques shop, but he refused."

"Interesting." He used the tongs to transfer the pasta from the pot into a colorful Italian pottery bowl then plopped slices of garlic bread into the bread basket and brought it all to the table. They took seats across from each other, and Lexy poured them each a glass of cabernet. Jack tucked his napkin into the neck of his shirt and asked, "Anything else?"

Lexy could barely keep the smile from her face. She was sure Jack didn't know about the valuable book. If he'd had an interesting clue like that, he would have already mentioned it. The book clue could crack the case wide open, and while she didn't want to seem as if she were trying to show him up, she was somewhat proud that she and the ladies had uncovered a clue the police might have missed.

"We found out that another copy of the same book Mary was giving away as a prize in the pie-eating contest sold on eBay a few weeks ago for ten thousand dollars. That would certainly give Lorelei ideas about making a small fortune, if she'd found the same information online that we did." Lexy took a sip of the rich, fruity wine. "By the way, did you take the book into evidence? If you did, you might want to make sure it's locked up."

"Book? We didn't take any book," Jack said around a bite of food. "I don't remember seeing one at the crime scene." Jack's brows mashed together, and Lexy could tell he was processing what she'd just told him.

"No one we talked to mentioned anything about a valuable book. Are you sure the one that sold on eBay is the same one that was being given as a prize?"

"Yep."

"And you guys didn't scour the senior center for it?"

"Not yet. We need to go back and do that. Mary kept it locked in the safe. We're hoping Sylvia will unlock it to see if it's still there." Lexy made a mental note.

Jack raised a brow but didn't say anything. She figured he was making the same mental note.

They chewed in silence for a few minutes, then Lexy remembered something else. "I meant to ask if you guys questioned the bartender at the party. We're trying to confirm that Chandler Bennington was at the bar the entire time just before I found Mary's body in the pie room."

"Of course we did. We have a protocol that we follow, and that includes methodical questioning of everyone who was there. You guys should try it sometime." Jack tempered his sarcasm with an indulgent smile. "The bartender thinks he remembers Chandler Bennington being there the whole time but couldn't swear to it. Apparently, the bar was pretty busy that night."

Lexy dug into her supper. The sauce was just the right mix of salty, spicy, and sweet, and the crunchy bread was to die for, as usual. They ate for a while in companionable silence while Sprinkles sat vigil near their feet, poised and ready to snatch anything that dropped.

Finally, Lexy sat back, took a sip of wine, and continued the conversation. "So, I told you what we discovered. What did you find out today?"

"Well, we didn't find anything in your pies." He winked at her over his wine glass. "But now, given what you just told me, I'm thinking our first theory might be wrong. We were originally thinking maybe a ring or earring or cuff link flew off when the killer was bludgeoning Mary. We still don't have a solid motive for anyone to want her dead. But if the motive was the book all along, and the book was locked up as you say, then maybe it was the key that fell into the pie and that's what the killer was looking for."

"Hmm. That makes sense. He followed Mary into the room, and they fought over the key. He clonked her. It flew into the pie. Then he grabbed the key, got the book, and ran out. But that still leaves the question of where the book is now. And there are other possible angles."

"Like what?"

Lexy forked up a grape tomato and popped it into her mouth. "We talked to Howard Archer today, you know, to give our condolences."

"Uh-huh."

"Anyway, several people at the party saw Howard carrying a present for Mary, and when we went to his house, I saw the discarded wrapping paper in the trash in his pantry. But when we asked him about it, he denied ever having a gift for his wife."

"We talked to Howard today too. He seemed quite distraught about Mary's death. He said he was in the poker game at the time," Jack said.

Lexy nodded. "There were also witnesses who said that Mary and Chandler had an argument at the party. He wanted to see her copy of his book, and she refused to show it to him, saying there wasn't time."

"Chandler did mention something about them not letting him see the book."

Jack got up to get a second serving. Lexy declined more food; she was stuffed.

He continued, "Sounds like they told us the same things. But it might not hurt to bring them in again to ask about the book and push them on their alibis."

"Better hurry," Lexy said, pouring herself more wine. "Chandler said he was leaving town in the morning."

"We'll see about that." Jack pulled out his cell phone and made a quick call to the station, asking them to send out an officer to inform Bennington that he was a person of interest in the case and that he wasn't allowed to leave Brook Ridge until the investigation into Mary Archer's death was completed. After he ended the call, he plunked his phone down on the table and grinned at Lexy. "Anything else you haven't told me yet, Sherlock?"

Lexy laughed. "No, but be sure to ask Chandler about the hallway situation when you bring him in. That's why the bartender's account is important—to see if he can place Chandler at the bar at the time of Mary's murder. Chandler said no one went down the hallway after Helen did, including Howard Archer. And before that, Helen was in the kitchen and didn't see anyone, so she's out as a witness. But a few people saw Howard with a gift, and Sylvia swears she saw Howard near the offices. So how did he get there without Chandler seeing him, and what happened to that gift?"

"Good questions." Jack shrugged, not looking up from his food. "Did you ever think that maybe the gift wasn't for Mary?"

"Ida did." Lexy watched him over the rim of her glass. "But with Helen in the kitchen and Chandler at the bar, how did the killer get out of the pie room without being noticed?"

Jack glanced up at Lexy, and she braced herself. He had that look in his eye. It was the look that came right before he told her to leave the investigating to the police. But this time, he didn't say that. Instead, his eyes softened, and he said, "I want you to promise me one thing."

"What?"

"You'll keep me filled in on what you find. And don't go confronting any suspects on your own."

"Okay." Lexy could see that Jack was genuinely concerned for her. She could hardly blame him for that. Besides, he hadn't forbidden her from investigating, and she'd take that as a victory.

Jack smiled. "That's my girl. So what do you think was the real motive? To get Mary out of the way, or to get this supposedly valuable book?"

Lexy sighed and sipped more wine. "I don't know, but I can say one thing: someone we've talked to is lying."

"When it comes to murder, honey," Jack said, wiping his mouth and then rising to clear the plates, "someone usually is."

CHAPTER TWELVE

*L*exy had just finished lining up the éclairs in a perfect row right next to the half-moon cookies in the bakery case at The Cup and Cake when she saw a flash of blue outside in the street. It was Nans and the ladies in Ruth's decades-old Oldsmobile. Pedestrians scattered as the car narrowly missed a fire hydrant while pulling up to the curb. She could barely see the top of Ruth's head sticking up from behind the wheel, her hands clutched at the ten o'clock and two o'clock positions. The big boat of a car was far too huge for Ruth to drive, but it held sentimental value, so she wouldn't give it up easily.

The ladies filed out of the car and marched inside, immediately crowding in front of the bakery case to pick out pastries, two for each. Well, except Helen, who was apparently sticking to her low-carb diet. Even Ida's persistence did not sway her resolve.

Lexy rang them up, and they settled in at one of the cafe tables at the window with steaming mugs of coffee in front of them. The bakery wasn't crowded at this time of day, so Lexy grabbed a cream horn and joined them, taking a small bite from the end of the horn that was mostly flaky pastry and just a bit of cream. She liked to eat the ends first and save the cream-stuffed middle for last.

Downtown Brook Ridge Falls was a quaint New England town with old brick mill buildings lining the river. The large front windows of The Cup and Cake looked out over the waterfall. Lexy could practically hear the water whooshing past as she watched it cascade over the rocks that made up the falls. Neat planters filled with blooming wildflowers in every shade dotted the sidewalks, and new wrought-iron street signs had been installed by the town to continue the picturesque feel.

The sound of a clasp snapping open drew Lexy's attention back inside, and she glanced over to see Helen rummaging through her huge handbag again. She half expected her to pull out more piecrust, but instead, she removed another tiny single-serving container of cottage cheese and a plastic spoon.

While the other ladies set about eating the luscious pastries set before them neatly on napkins, Helen ate her cottage cheese, making an elaborate show of moaning in delight as she licked the spoon and exclaimed how tasty it was. Lexy liked healthy food as much as the next person, but there was no way Helen's snack compared to the freshly made cupcakes, Danish, and scones.

Ida rolled her eyes and grinned at Lexy, obviously agreeing.

Helen saw their exchanged looks and was not amused. She arched a brow at Lexy before turning to Ida beside her and scowling. "My breakfast is only one hundred fifty calories. How much fat and sugar are in that scone of yours, Ida?"

"Who cares?" Ida said around another mouthful of butterscotch chip scone, the crystalized sugar and caramel topping coating her lips. "It's delicious."

Nans shook her head and patted Lexy's hand. "Don't pay any attention to Helen, dear. She's not thinking clearly due to lack of fuel to her brain."

Helen stuck her tongue out at Nans, which Nans ignored as she continued.

"Do tell us, dear. Did Jack mention anything new on the investigation into Mary's death?"

"Not really, no." Lexy popped more of her cream

horn into her mouth and took a sip of coffee. "He did say that Howard told them he'd been playing poker at the time his wife was killed, the same as he told us. Oh, and he said the police never found any book near the body. And the police did ask the bartender if Chandler Bennington was there the whole time, but he couldn't remember."

"Thank you, dear." Nans dusted Danish crumbs from her hands and looked around the table with a smile. "So I take it the police didn't know about the value of the book, then?"

"Nope." Lexy sipped more coffee as the ladies exchanged knowing glances.

"I'm sure they will be looking into that further now," Ruth said.

"No doubt," Lexy replied. "Jack also said they didn't find any clues in the pies they confiscated either."

"Oh, that is good news!" Ida perked up at that tidbit. "Does that mean they'll release the pies soon?"

Everyone gave her a funny look.

Lexy made a face. "Ida, even if they did, you don't want to eat those things. They've been handled by goodness knows who, and by now, they must be stale. If you want a pie that bad, I'll make you one."

"Such a waste." Ida scoffed. "And silly too. I bet

some of them are still good. And I'd only eat the parts no one had touched anyway." She shifted in her seat to lean closer to Lexy. "Do you think you could talk Jack into getting me those pies? I hate to see you put in extra work just to make me a new one."

Helen gave her a disgusted look. "The last thing you need, Ida, is more pie."

"What do you mean?" Ida sat back and glared at her friend. "You got a problem with my eating habits?"

"Well, now that you mention it..." Helen said, her tone rising.

"Ida, dear," Ruth said, entering the fray. "We didn't want to mention anything, but you have put on a little weight lately."

"Excuse me?" Ida made a show of looking herself up and down, her expression sour. Honestly, if she had put on weight, Lexy couldn't see it. She was still just as petite as usual, but the ladies did enjoy getting her dander up. "I am not fat!"

"Actually," Ruth said, "you are getting a bit soft in the middle."

"I'll give you soft in the middle," Ida growled, raising her fist in defiance.

Helen snorted. "Maybe you could try the low-carb diet too. I've lost ten pounds already."

"Yeah?" Ida narrowed her gaze. "Well, maybe you could try..."

"Enough about that," Nans cut in, defusing the situation by standing and clearing away their trash. "I say we get back to the community center and find that missing book. If it's still in the safe in Mary's office, then we can rule that out as a motive for the murder. Lexy, dear, do you have time to come with us?"

Lexy glanced over at Cassie behind the counter. She hated to ditch her twice in two days, but Cassie had told Lexy that she liked running the bakery by herself sometimes. It gave her time to think, she said. And it was the middle of the week, so the place wouldn't be really busy. From behind the counter, Cassie gave Lexy a nod and wink of approval.

"Uh, sure," Lexy said. "Okay. Let me just take off my apron and make sure Cassie has everything she needs."

While Lexy whipped off her apron and headed toward Cassie, Nans and the ladies headed back outside to Ruth's giant blue Oldsmobile, still bickering about Ida's girth.

CHAPTER THIRTEEN

*T*he ride to the community center in Ruth's Oldsmobile was as harrowing as usual. There was a reason Lexy usually drove, even though Ruth's car was much roomier. Ruth hit every pothole and veered onto every curb as she maneuvered the big boat of a car slowly along the streets of Brook Ridge Falls. At least Ida wasn't driving. When she drove, it was more like driving on the track of the Indy 500 than on the back roads of a small town.

There were no parties or functions, and it was too early for bingo or a group gathering to watch *Wheel of Fortune*, so the community center parking lot was empty except for a small blue Toyota. Ruth still insisted on parking perfectly, backing up and inching

LEIGHANN DOBBS

forward four or five times to make sure she was lined up in the space.

"That's Sylvia Hensel's car," Ruth said. "She gave me a ride to the pharmacy once when the Olds was in storage for the winter."

"Good. We'll get to talk to her alone," Nans said as she pushed open the door, ignoring the metallic groan it made. They headed down the hallway toward the offices, meeting Sylvia, who was on her way out.

"Oh, I'm sorry," Sylvia said. She was dressed in a smart black pantsuit with a pretty green top. Still the same pearl necklace that she always wore, but diamond earrings sparkled in her ears instead of the usual pearls. "I was just on my way out. I really can't talk to you right now."

"Please." Nans didn't budge, blocking Sylvia's way, though her smile remained polite. "Please. We only have a few more questions. It won't take long."

Sylvia sighed and gestured for Nans to go into the office, her expression as reluctant as her tone. "Yes, all right. But make it quick. I have places to go and things to do."

"Perfect," Nans said as the rest of them crowded into the tiny space. Nans and Helen took the two available remaining seats, while everyone else stood behind them, facing Sylvia. The office was perhaps ten by ten, with a wraparound desk with upper shelves built in. It took up at least half the space, leaving little room for anything else. The walls and carpet were bland beige, and there was one framed photo on the wall of a Paris street scene. Nothing remarkable. The desktop itself overflowed with papers and stacks of binders.

"Okay," Nans continued, balancing her purse on her lap. "We want to know what happened to the book that was the prize for the pie-eating contest."

"What about it?" Sylvia asked, frowning.

"Do you know where it is now?" Helen asked.

"Well, Mary always kept it locked in her office safe. I told her it was silly. The book was only worth a quarter, but she said that was where she always kept the prizes. I could see her keeping the Cactus Joe's vouchers there. At least *those* were worth something. Anyway, I assume that's where it still is." Sylvia seemed confused, frowning. "Why?"

"Do you know if she had the book with her right before she was murdered?" Lexy crossed her arms, cutting to the chase. Perhaps it was the kerfuffle with Ida and her weight, but Lexy was feeling a bit feisty. "You said she went to her office to get the contest trophy. Was it possible she grabbed the book from her safe while she was in there too?"

"I-I don't know." Sylvia sat back, her face pale.

"I'm not sure I understand what that old book has to do with anything anyway."

"A lot, we're guessing," Ida said. "That's why we need to pinpoint what's happened to it."

"Can you tell us everything you remember about the moments leading up to Mary's body being found in the pie room?" Nans said. "You said you were talking with Mary in her office. Think back. Do you recall if she had the book with her?"

Sylvia shook her head. "I'm not sure. I wasn't really paying attention."

"Where is her safe?" Ruth asked. "Can we see it? Are you able to open it?"

Sylvia nodded and pulled a key on a blue ribbon from her drawer before standing. She led them next door to Mary's office. While the rooms were approximately the same size with the same type of desks, Mary's space, by contrast, was clean and tidy, everything seemingly in its place. The walls and carpet were done in a cheerful shade of warm mauve, and there were numerous photos of Mary and Howard, and people Lexy assumed were their children and grandchildren.

Sylvia walked to the safe mounted at shoulder level in the wall opposite Mary's desk. Lexy held her breath as Sylvia unlocked the safe and opened the door wide so they could all see inside.

"It's empty!" Nans proclaimed.

Sylvia peered inside. "Why, that's odd. I could have sworn it would be there." She looked around the room.

"Does anyone else have a key to this safe?" Ruth asked, peering inside the empty space. She used to be involved with mobsters and the like—if anyone would be familiar with the inside of a safe, it would be Ruth.

"There are only two keys. Mary always wore one around her neck when she was working." Sylvia's voice caught on a tiny sob.

"Is that hers?" Ruth pointed to the key strung on a blue ribbon.

Sylvia frowned at the key. "This? Oh no. This is the extra from security. I guess Mary's was still around her neck when..."

"There, there." Helen patted her shoulder, giving the rest of the group a glance. "Seems Mary took the center's security quite seriously."

"Yes, she did." Sylvia sniffled. "She was president, after all."

"I didn't know her that well," Lexy said, sympathy for the grieving woman pinching her heart. "But when I met with her about the catering for the party, Mary struck me as a stickler for keeping things orderly and safe. She mentioned the key pads on the doors for entry and how she would assign Cassie and me temporary cards that would be good for the day of the party only, so we could get everything set up ahead of time if the place was locked. She said that while they'd let the cameras fall by the wayside, she'd made sure to keep up with the access codes. Said she never gave them out to anyone and instructed all her staff and the members to do the same. She also mentioned the windows were always locked. I'd asked about using them to cool the pies that day, but it wasn't an option."

"She always had everyone else's best interests at heart. Poor woman." Nans shook her head then took the key from Sylvia's hand and held it up by the ribbon. "So, is this the master key, then?"

"Yes." Sylvia exhaled slowly, staring down at her toes. "As I said, because Mary is ... gone ... I figured I should keep this one handy until I get hers back from the police. I imagine it must be in her personal effects that went to Howard."

They went back to Sylvia's office, and Nans took her seat again while the rest of them gathered behind her. Ida and Ruth leaned against the wall near the hallway. "The last time we spoke to you, Sylvia, you mentioned seeing Howard in the hallway during your conversation with Mary. Is there any chance you might have been mistaken?"

"I don't think so," Sylvia said, pulling out some tissues to dab her nose. "Why?"

"Chandler Bennington and Howard are about the same height and build," Ida said. She made a show of peering out into the rather dimly lit hallway. "Do you think you could've gotten the two confused?"

"No." Sylvia's tone was adamant. "I'm sure it was Howard. I even saw him again from the kitchen when I went in there after finishing with Mary."

"Why were you in the kitchen?" Lexy asked, bristling. Lexy liked things to be a certain way during her catering events. She organized the kitchen to run smoothly, and she'd had problems before with clients getting into the kitchen and messing things up. Mary had promised during their meeting about the catering that no one but Cassie and she would have been in that area.

"Oh." She gave Lexy a sheepish look. "Don't worry, Lexy. It had nothing to do with your wonderful pies. I just wanted to make sure no one had left the ovens on by accident. Mary had told me not to go in there, but I worry."

"And that's when you saw Howard in the hall?" Nans persisted.

"Yes." Sylvia twisted the tissue in her hands. "I mean, I didn't pass him directly, but I saw a shadowed figure about his size pass by the doorway. I'm certain it was him."

"How can you be sure it wasn't Chandler Bennington?" Helen asked, narrowing her gaze. "He was bothering Mary about seeing that book, wasn't he?

Sylvia shrugged again. "Yes, he was quite insistent about it, but I don't think he'd be bold enough to come down the hall. Everyone knew it was off limits until the pie-eating contest began."

"Do you think he was interested enough to try to get a look at it himself, without Mary?" Helen continued with the interrogation.

"As I said, I really don't know." Sylvia threw up her hands in exasperation. "I'm not familiar with him or his books. I'm sorry." She frowned. "Can one of you please explain to me why some novel Mary bought at a rummage sale is worth all this fuss?"

"We have reason to believe the book had some value," Nans said vaguely before asking another question of her own. "So, you saw a figure you presumed to be Howard Archer in the hallway while you were checking the kitchens you weren't supposed to be in. What did you do after that, Sylvia?"

Cheeks flushed, Sylvia huffed. "I already told you

that I went back to the main dining room to make sure everything was set for the pie-eating contest. Why do I feel like I'm on trial here?"

"Did you go speak to Chandler Bennington as instructed?" Nans asked, ignoring her belligerent attitude.

"Yes." Sylvia crossed her arms and sat back, her expression annoyed. "I already told you that too."

"Where was he during your conversation?" Ruth asked.

"At the bar." Her nose wrinkled with distaste. "And he'd already had a few too many, if you ask me. Barely did more than grunt at me when I asked him about his presentation. I didn't want to linger, but then I didn't have to. That's when Lexy came in and made the terrible announcement about poor Mary." Her face crumpled again, and tears slid down her face. She pushed to her feet and made her way to the door, where she stood to give them a pointed stare. "Now, if you don't mind, I have an appointment to keep."

Sylvia ushered everyone out of her office then locked the door behind her before walking away without a backward glance.

Nans waited until the woman was out of earshot before saying, "Something doesn't add up here. The timing's off with what everyone told us. Sylvia says she talked to Chandler at the bar after she saw Howard a second time in the hallway because she'd gone to check on the kitchens, where she never should've been in the first place. But if Chandler killed Mary, he would've passed Howard in the hallway too, right?"

"Or if it was the other way around and Howard is the killer. Then Chandler would've seen Howard from where he was sitting at the bar. But he denied seeing anyone but me," Helen said.

"Not to mention that Helen didn't see Howard or Sylvia or Chandler," Nans said.

"There's one way to find out for sure," Ruth said. "Let's perform a reenactment to determine exactly how everything took place and work out the timing ourselves."

CHAPTER FOURTEEN

"Good thing bingo doesn't start for two hours. We have the whole place to ourselves," Nans said as they stood in the empty dining room. "Now, where should we start?"

"We need to figure out if all the suspects were indeed where they said they were," Ruth said. "My money is on Chandler Bennington, so maybe we should start with when Helen saw him at the bar."

Nans pressed her lips together. "No, I think that's too late. Anyone know what he was doing before that?"

"I brought him a piece of pie before that. When he was still at the table," Lexy said.

Nans's left brow ticked up. "Oh? And then what happened?"

Lexy closed her eyes, remembering the sequence

of events after she brought Chandler the pie. "He refused it then took off for the bar. I watched him go. Cassie asked if I wanted to give the pie room one more look before the contest, so I dropped off my tray in the corner. That's when I noticed Helen standing in the hallway near the entrance by the bar."

"And then you went to the pie room?" Ida asked.

"Yes. No, wait ... before that, I lit the burner under the chafing dish for the scalloped potatoes." Lexy opened her eyes and looked at Ruth. "Remember? The potatoes had gone cold."

"I certainly do."

"Might be a blessing in disguise," Helen said. "Those things are loaded with carbs."

"Anyway," Nans cut in, "how long did it take you to light that burner?"

"Just a few seconds."

"And then you headed straight to the pie room?"

"Yes."

"Good," Nans said. "Now, Helen, you'd just come from the kitchen. How long would you guess you were in there?"

"I'd estimate maybe five minutes." Helen shrugged. "I pilfered crust from Lexy's rejected pies, but I didn't want to be obvious about it, so I made my selections carefully. And I was afraid of getting caught, so I stuffed all of it into my handbag fast. When I was done, I didn't linger."

"And you didn't see anyone coming down the hallway while you were in there?" Nans asked.

"No." Helen's cheeks flushed as she stared down at her toes. "But I'll admit I was more focused on getting those carbs than anything else. Given that I could hear Mary and Sylvia in their offices, they must've passed by me at some point. Their offices are just down the hall from the kitchens. But I wasn't paying attention."

"So, it's conceivable you might have missed seeing Howard lurking out there?" Ruth asked.

"That's right." Helen straightened a bit. "I could have."

"All right," Nans said. "Helen, you got your piecrusts. Then what did you do?"

"I hightailed it out of there, stopped near the bar to decide what to do, then figured the ladies' room was the best place, so I hurried over there," Helen said.

"When you stopped near the entrance to the main dining room, do you remember seeing Chandler Bennington at the bar?" Lexy asked.

"I think so, yes."

"Good." Nans turned to Lexy. "Now, Lexy, you said you spotted Helen in the hallway after Chandler walked away from your pie. What did you do then?"

"I lit the burner under the scalloped potatoes, then Cassie and I went to make sure everything was ready for the contest."

"And how long did that take for you to discover Mary's body?" Nans asked.

"Not long. Maybe a minute at most from the time we walked into the pie room."

Nans sighed and pursed her lips. "So, most likely, Mary's killer had just escaped after killing her."

"That doesn't give him much time to commit murder and go down the hallway," Ida said. "It would have to have been someone who knew where Mary was going to be, right? And he would've had to be able to blend in with the rest of the crowd afterward without drawing suspicion. He had to have exited the hallway while Lexy was lighting the burners."

"Good point," Nans said.

"Could Chandler have brushed off Sylvia and slipped into the pie room to kill Mary while Lexy was at the buffet? Maybe he was tracking Mary's movements, and when Sylvia came up to him, he knew Mary would be alone," Ruth offered.

Helen snapped her fingers. "And if he had been watching the hallway from his vantage point at the bar —which we know he was because he ratted me out—

then he would have known Mary was down there alone."

"We know he was already upset because she wouldn't let him see the book. Helen said she was too preoccupied with her carbs to pay much attention to anything other than getting to the ladies' room, so she wouldn't have noticed where he was or what he was doing after she passed the bar." Ida looked over at Lexy. "You weren't watching him either. Were you, Lexy?"

"No." Lexy shook her head. "Cassie and I had our hands full with cleaning up after dinner service and making sure things were ready to go for the pie-eating contest."

"So, what did you see when you first walked into the pie room?" Nans asked.

"Not much. The lights were off, so it was pretty dark in there. The sun must've been behind a cloud, because there wasn't much light coming in through the curtained windows." Lexy frowned. "At first, everything seemed fine. Then Cassie pointed out that someone must've started already because it looked like someone had already been eating one of the pies. That's when I went over to see who it was and found Mary."

"Do you remember seeing anyone else besides

LEIGHANN DOBBS

Helen in the hallway when you walked across to the pie room, Lexy?" Nans asked.

"Nope. Just Helen."

Nans exhaled slowly. "And what did you do once you found Mary's body?"

"Like I said, the room was relatively dark when we first walked in, so I only saw that someone was slumped over one of the pies, not who it was. I tapped her on the shoulder, thinking perhaps she hadn't heard me, and that's when the body fell to the floor. Cassie turned on the light, and we saw that it was Mary Archer and that she was dead." Lexy shuddered. "I called Jack immediately and secured the scene, as he'd taught me. Then I left Cassie to guard the area while I went down the hall to announce in the main dining room that the contest was canceled."

"Right." Nans turned to Ruth, their official time-keeper. "So, let's walk out Lexy's route."

Ruth whipped out her smartphone and set the timer. They then disappeared into the main dining room, reappearing moments later.

"How long?" Nans asked.

"Not long," Ruth said, frowning. "I calculate there was a five-minute window for the killer to sneak into the pie room, kill Mary, then get out again. Give or take a minute or two either way."

"And it had to have been someone people were used to seeing around here or expected, because they didn't draw attention to themselves, right?" Ida asked.

"True," Nans said. "But then again, no one was really paying that much attention. Helen said she was too focused on getting to the bathroom to eat her carbs, and Lexy and Cassie were busy preparing for the contest. Everyone else was partying."

"Chandler could still have done it," Helen said. "He was close by, at the bar. He could've slipped away after Sylvia left and clonked Mary over the head. It would take only a second if she didn't struggle."

"But what if she did? And what about looking for the book?" Nans asked. "It just doesn't seem like enough time to do all that *and* get back down the hall-way. Plus, what did the killer do with the book? No one saw anyone with it."

"Or maybe no one noticed. Everyone was more concerned with the murder," Lexy pointed out.

"Well, the only person mentioned being in the hall already was Howard, but Ruth said she saw Howard at the poker game, so he has an alibi too."

"Um, about that," Ruth said, fidgeting slightly. "I'm not so sure about what I said."

"What?" Nans scowled. "Why?"

"Well, I *had* been playing poker. That's true. But

then I got hungry, and I remembered those delicious scalloped potatoes on the buffet, so I went to get some before everything was cleared away." She lifted one shoulder. "Based on the timeline we've just laid out, I wasn't in the poker room at the time that Mary was killed. I was in the main dining room, so I couldn't really verify where Howard Archer was during the murder." She narrowed her gaze. "But I do know who could tell us if he was in the poker room when his wife was killed—Rena Wakowski. She stayed in there all night because she was winning."

"Oh Lord!" Helen cringed. "Please, not her."

"Well, then." Nans smoothed a hand down the front of her cream-colored cardigan. "Looks like we'll be paying Rena a visit next."

CHAPTER FIFTEEN

*R*ena Wakowski lived in the same apartment building as Nans, just one floor down. That made it pretty convenient, so Helen texted ahead, and then Lexy and the ladies stopped off at Nans's for some fortifying coffee before following the brown indoor-outdoor carpeting down the hall to the stairs and down one floor.

They stopped in front of unit 108, and Helen tapped on the white-painted door.

Rena stood about five feet two, with a grizzled face and wiry gray hair. She seemed the type of tough gal who would be as comfortable in the ring with Rocky as she would teaching kickboxing to seniors at the community center, which she did every Thursday at six p.m. In fact, she reminded Lexy of those weight-loss coaches on reality TV, the ones who screamed at their clients until they cried then called it tough love.

She greeted Helen at the door like a comrade. The rest of them? Not so much.

"You look great, kid," Rena said to Helen, eyeing her up and down. "How are you doing with your eating?" Her expression hardened. "Did you cheat?"

"What? No." Helen cast a nervous glance at all of them. Nans's left brow ticked up. Ida smirked. But no one said a word about Helen's piecrust indiscretion. "Of course I didn't cheat. May we come in for a moment?"

"Uh," Rena gave them the once-over before moving aside to clear the doorway. "Sure, I guess. What are you all doing here? Want to start on my low-carb diet plan too?"

"No," Nans said, and Rena visibly deflated. "But we do have a couple of questions for you, if that's all right."

Rena shrugged and led them through her apartment to the eat-in kitchen. The layout was virtually the same as Nans's except reversed. She even had a similar mahogany dining room table.

Her kitchen had a round maple table. Lexy was surprised to see a delicious-looking coffee cake in the middle of the table. Ida's eyes lit up in surprise when she spied it. But instead of offering them all a slice, Rena plated up slices of turkey breast and avocado. Ida's disappointment was palpable.

"You ought to think about starting a low-carb section in that bakery of yours, Lexy," Rena said as she handed her a plate and a fork. "I'm telling you girls, it's all the rage in the big cities. Bet you it's gonna come here too and get real popular. Just you wait and see. Low carb will drive shops like yours right out of business."

Her blunt statement took Lexy by surprise. "Oh, I don't think that will happen. There's room for both types of goods in the marketplace." Wasn't there?

"If you say so." Rena took a seat at the table across from Lexy, her small smile taunting.

Lexy chewed her tasteless turkey and avocado and started to worry. What would she do if The Cup and Cake went under? Jack made a decent salary as a detective, but they couldn't survive on his salary alone. Nah, she was being silly. This low-carb stuff was for the birds. She could tell by the way Ida, Ruth, and Nans were trying to choke down the turkey to be polite. People would always want sugary pastries, even if some did switch to a low-carb lifestyle.

"Well," Nans said, pushing aside her half-eaten food. "That was a lovely snack, but I'm afraid we're not interested in going on low-carb diets. What we wanted to talk to you about, Rena, was Mary Archer's death."

"Oh Lord!" Rena wiped her mouth and shook her head. "Such nasty business."

"Yes, it is." Nans leaned forward to rest her elbows on the table. "Specifically, we want to know if you remember seeing Mary's husband, Howard, in the poker room with you that night, especially around the time of her death." Nans glanced over at Ruth. "We have it on good authority that you were playing most of the night."

"Yeah, I was." Rena snorted. "When you're on a roll, you're on a roll, right?"

"Right." Nans frowned. "About Howard, though?"

"Yeah, yeah." Rena reached over and plucked a piece of untouched turkey off Nans's plate, rolled it up, and popped it in her mouth. "I'll tell you. This new low-carb diet, in addition to making me lose a ton of weight, has also sharpened my mind. Nothing gets past me anymore."

"I'll bet," Ida whispered. Ruth snorted.

Nans gave them each a stern look before turning back to Rena. "Go on."

"Let's see. We started that first hand of poker around six fifteen. Howard was there, then. So were Ruth and I, of course. Oh, and Benny Sullivan, Ed

Rourke, Gertie Flanders, Skip and Hettie Carlson, Bud Dixon, and the Johnsons. You remember all of them, right, Ruth?"

Ruth nodded. "I lost a bundle to Skip but luckily won it back in a big pot."

"That hand was crazy." Rena grinned. "Bud folded after that and left. Skip ended up running out of money. Then you left too, Ruth. Said you needed to take a break." Rena finished her last bite of avocado then sat back. "Howard left a few minutes after you did. Next thing I remember after that was Lexy making her announcement about the contest being canceled."

"So, Howard left before Lexy's announcement?" Ruth asked, her gaze darting to Nans.

"Yep. It was quite a while before. We played another hand, in fact. I got bored sitting there by myself, so I got up to run to my car to get myself a low-carb energy bar. They don't have enough low-carb offerings at these things. Caterers should take that into consideration." Her eyes slid to Lexy. "Anyway, that's when I saw Howard arguing with Lorelei Summers."

Nans's brows shot up at that. "Howard and Lorelei were arguing? What about?"

Lexy exchanged a look with Nans. Howard wasn't

in the poker game as he'd claimed. Either he'd forgotten about leaving the game, or he'd lied.

"Darned if I know," Rena said, standing up to clear their plates. "But whatever it was, it looked pretty heated."

The ladies exchanged a look, and Helen hopped up to help Rena, who nodded her approval at Helen. She looked over her shoulder at Lexy and the ladies as she scraped food into the garbage can. "See there? Helen has the energy and vitality to help clean up because she's not bogged down with carbs. You ladies might take a lesson from her. Especially you, Lexy. You're too young to be slumped at the table in a carb-induced stupor."

Lexy immediately straightened. Had she been slumping?

Rena dashed to the hutch and picked up some stapled papers and handed them out to the women. "Now this here is what I call my starter diet. It will ease you in. It's not that hard. Right, Helen?" She glanced at Helen, who nodded.

"Anyway, see, you gotta make sure you get lots of fats too. That will keep you satiated." She pointed to the top of the paper.

"Uh ... thanks." Ida grabbed her paper and stood. "How much fat is in a doughnut?"

Rena scowled. "I don't find that at all funny."

"I bet an éclair has more. It's that custard filling." Ida smirked.

Helen cleared her throat and grabbed Ida by the elbow, steering her toward the door. "Well, it was lovely talking to you, but Ida has a proctologist appointment, and she can't be late."

"Oh, low-carb will help with that too! Lots of vegetables." Rena patted her stomach. "Keeps you regular and your guts in good working order."

Lexy, Nans, and Ruth had jumped up from the table while they had the chance and were hurrying to the door behind Helen and Ida.

"Thanks for answering our questions, Rena," Nans called as they rushed out into the hallway.

"Well, that certainly was interesting about Howard," Ruth said as they walked down the hallway back to Nans's.

"Indeed," Nans said. "He clearly must have lied."

"Or maybe he simply forgot where he was—if he left the poker game just for a minute or two," Helen suggested.

"Maybe," Lexy said. "But what about the argument? Why would he argue with Lorelei?"

"Do you think it could be related to the argument she had with Chandler?" Ida asked.

"Or Chandler's argument with Mary?" Lexy added.

"I'm not sure, but there's one thing I am sure of: the book is missing, and there's one person who certainly would have known the value," Nans said. "Looks like we need to pay a visit to Lorelei's antiques shop."

CHAPTER SIXTEEN

*L*exy talked the ladies into waiting until midafternoon to visit Lorelei and headed to the bakery, glad she was driving her own car and not being chauffeured in Ruth's. The bakery tended to get busy at lunchtime, and she helped Cassie sell cookies, cupcakes, and brownies to the lunch-dessert crowd. She filled Cassie in on the case during the lulls.

"Jack said they didn't find anything in the pies." The last of the lunchtime rush customers were gone, and Cassie had her head in the bakery case, rear-ranging after the crush of customers practically depleted the supply of chocolate chip cookies.

"Mary's key seems to be missing. And the book is

gone too, so I guess the killer found what he was looking for in the pies."

"The key?"

"Yep."

"So you think it was Chandler? Why would he steal his own book back?"

Lexy sprayed the glass on the pastry case with a mixture of vinegar and water and started wiping with a cloth. The case had dozens of fingerprints from customers pointing out their selections. She liked it to be clear and shiny. "It could be Howard too. He lied about where he was when Mary was killed, and he was seen arguing with Lorelei."

Cassie frowned. "About what?"

"No idea." Lexy stood back to make sure the glass was clear and streak free.

"The disappearance of the book is very suspicious. Does Jack know about that?" Cassie asked.

Lexy smiled. "He does now. Nans sort of broke the case on that one. He didn't even know the book was valuable until I told him Ruth had looked it up. Anyway, after Sylvia opened the safe at the community center and we realized the book wasn't in it, I texted Jack to keep him in the loop."

"Good thing. Can't have Nans and the ladies

getting ahead of the cops now, can we?" Cassie pulled a cannoli out, broke it in half, and gave one half to Lexy. "One thing, though—my cousin used to collect books, and they aren't all valued the same. For example, a first edition would be worth a lot more than a later edition, so the book Mary had might not have been valuable at all. Signatures do add to the value."

"Good point. Which reminds me..." Lexy shoved the rest of the cannoli in her mouth and reached for her purse. "There's one person who should be well versed in the value of old books: Lorelei Summers. And it just so happens I have a date to pick up Nans and the ladies to pay Lorelei a little visit."

Fifteen minutes later, the ladies were wedged into Lexy's VW, pulling up in front of Lorelei's antiques store. It was situated in a quaint old house just off the main drag. A hand-carved sign swung from the porch rafters, proclaiming the name of the store in gold letters on a black background: Hidden Treasures Antiques and Collectibles.

The shop was packed from floor to ceiling with all manner of knickknacks and bric-a-brac. Occupational hazard, Lexy supposed. Lorelei had been in business at this location for years and must have collected quite a bit of stuff.

Lorelei was behind the counter, ringing up customers, when they arrived, so they looked around for a while until she was free. She was a pleasant-looking woman in her late sixties, short and curvy. She always reminded Lexy of an old hippie with her long white hair, colorful tie-dyed shirts, and faded jeans. The patchouli incense she had smoldering by the register added to the effect.

She finally drifted out from behind her register and over to them in the corner of the store designated for old coins and toys. "Mona. Ladies, what can I do for you today?"

She seemed pleasant, serene. Lexy half expected her to flash them a peace sign.

Nans gave her a polite smile. "We wanted to ask you a few questions about the book that Mary Archer was going to give away as the prize for the pie-eating contest. How much it was worth."

"Oh." Lorelei fussed with a pile of old wooden blocks on the table. "I don't think I'll be much help to you, then. Sorry. I don't know anything about the value of old or rare books."

"But this is an antiques store," Ruth said, frowning. "It's your business to know, isn't it?"

"About the things I sell regularly, yes." Lorelei shrugged. "But I only know the types of items I normally deal in. Silver, Limoges china, old dolls. Everything else, I only have rudimentary knowledge about. There's just too much to know, and I still do everything by hand. No technology. Don't believe in it." To prove her point, she reached into the pocket of her loose caftan and pulled out an old cordless phone handset. "See? I don't even have a cell phone. Still use the landline. Even my cash register is manual. No electricity."

"Huh." Ida wrinkled her nose. "What about a computer? Inventory? How do you survive in this day and age when everything's on the Internet?"

Lorelei scoffed. "I've been in business for decades, honey. I don't need to be plugged in to do what I do."

"Lorelei, I hate to bring this up, but we've been told that you argued with Howard Archer just before Mary was killed. Is that true?" Helen asked, staying firmly in the middle of the walkway to avoid brushing her navy-blue polyester slacks against any of the dusty relics in the store.

"Me? Argue with Howard? About what?" She shook her head, frowning. "No, he's such a nice man, I can't imagine ever disagreeing with him about anything. But that Chandler Bennington, he's a different story altogether." She scrunched her nose. "If you're looking for suspects in Mary's death, he's one you should be talking to. Not a nice man at all. Why, he wouldn't even sign any of my books."

"And why exactly did you want them signed?" Nans's gaze narrowed. "You just said you had no idea of their value."

"Oh, I don't." Lorelei gave a dismissive wave. "But the tourists love signed books. They sell very well, regardless of the author or their value."

"So, you're telling us you didn't talk to Howard Archer at all then, before the pie-eating contest?" Lexy asked, a knot in her gut telling her something wasn't right about Lorelei's story.

"Look, I'm telling you Chandler Bennington is the one you should be looking at," Lorelei said, her normally sweet tone turning decidedly defensive. "Howard Archer wouldn't harm a fly. That writer, on the other hand, is mean and petty. It would've taken him two seconds to scribble his signature in my books, yet he couldn't be bothered. I mean, who acts that way?"

The ladies and Lexy exchanged a look.

Nans stepped forward. "Do you have any idea who might have wanted to kill Mary Archer?"

"What? No." Lorelei moved back, bumping into the table behind her and toppling the set of carefully stacked wooden blocks. She picked them up, skirted around the table, and headed back behind her register. "Why would I have any idea? I didn't know the woman that well, and there were a lot of people at the party that day. I have no idea. Not sure why you'd even ask me."

More customers came in, and Lorelei escaped to wait on them. Lexy and the ladies headed for the door. At the last second, Nans turned back and asked Lorelei, "Where were you when Lexy made her announcement about the contest being canceled?"

Lorelei's cheeks reddened. "I don't have to tell you ladies anything." She flashed a pained smile at her other customers before glaring at the ladies and hissing, "If you must know, I was at the front door, helping Sylvia Hensel get the extra bibs for the contest entrants."

"Thank you," Nans said, leading the group outside. The ladies said nothing until about half a block from the store. While they waited at the corner for traffic, Nans looked at Lexy, frowning. "That was an odd conversation."

"You're telling me," Ida piped in. "Talk about defensive."

"Hmm," Ruth agreed. "Sounds like she's got something to hide."

"I don't remember Sylvia mentioning anything

about being at the front door with the bibs when Lexy made the announcement," Nans said.

"I thought she was with Chandler," Ida said.

"Me too," Lexy said. "But if she wasn't, then maybe that's the hole in Chandler's alibi."

CHAPTER SEVENTEEN

*O*n the way back to the community center, Lexy remembered her promise to Jack. They'd done a lot of investigating that afternoon, and she'd promised to keep him apprised.

"It's still early. Why don't we stop in and share what we've learned with Jack?" Lexy suggested.

The ladies were all over that, of course. They never passed up an opportunity to snoop around inside law enforcement's headquarters.

"Yeah, maybe we can get some insider information," Ruth said.

"Something Jack didn't even tell Lexy," Ida suggested. "Ruth could hypnotize him and get him to tell some secret info on the case."

"I don't think we need to stoop to that," Nans said.

LEIGHANN DOBBS

"Jack is usually pretty good with sharing. We just need to do our part and fill him in on what we have learned."

It was a quiet day on the crime front, apparently. The front lobby was empty, and even the receptionist looked bored. She waved them back to see Jack without hesitation. There wasn't much crime in Brook Ridge Falls aside from the dead bodies Lexy stumbled onto every so often.

Jack was in his office, staring at a stack of files on his desk. His handsome face lit up when Lexy stuck her head inside.

"Hey, honey," Jack said, getting up and walking over to give her a kiss on the cheek. "To what do I owe this pleasure?"

Lexy moved aside so the ladies could file into his small office then closed the door behind them. Jack's brows rose at the four ladies all lined up on one side of his office, all wearing their serious detective faces. He leaned his hip against the desk, his lips quirked in amusement.

"Ladies, I assume you have something for me."

Nans nodded. "We've been out talking to people about Mary Archer's death, and we thought we'd stop in and share what we've found out with you."

"Perfect." Jack walked back behind his old metal

desk, took a seat, and leaned forward, resting his elbows on the pen-marked surface. "Lay it on me, ladies."

Nans relayed everything they'd learned so far. The fact that the book was missing from the safe. The tip they'd gotten from Rena concerning Howard lying about where he was and his argument with Lorelei. The odd way Lorelei had acted. And finally, their reenactment earlier that day.

"So you see, Howard lied about being in the poker game. I'm sure he knew exactly where he was when Lexy made that announcement. I mean, who wouldn't remember exactly where they were when finding out something like that?"

"Yeah, I figured that out too," Jack said.

"And the missing book is suspicious. The killer likely has that key." Nans turned to Jack. "Or have you found it?"

"Nope. We didn't find anything in the pies."

Ida sighed at the mention of the pies.

Jack turned to Lexy. "Everyone did say they looked delicious, if that's any comfort. And perfectly cooled despite how hot the air is outside. They would have been perfect for the contest."

"We just came from Lorelei Summers's shop," Ruth added. "And I think she knows something."

"She said she was in front, helping Sylvia with the bibs, when the announcement was made. If that's true, I don't think she could have done it, according to the timing in our walk-through. She wouldn't be able to go from the hallway to the front door without being seen by one of us."

"I'll make a note to talk to Sylvia and verify that." Jack scribbled something down on a pad of paper.

"And I'm still very suspicious of Chandler Bennington," Nans said.

"Nope." Jack's chair squeaked as he leaned back. "No dice there. Sorry, Mona. We've cleared Chandler already. He has debilitating arthritis in his joints, including his fingers. There's no way he could've held that trophy, let alone produced enough force to hit Mary over the head with it hard enough to kill her. I saw his hands. They're so gnarled he can't even straighten his fingers."

"Must be hard to write with gnarled hands," Ruth said.

"Not to mention sign books," Nans added.

"Guess that explains why he kept them hidden all the time," Lexy said. "Now that I remember, he always had them in his pockets. I guess that was because he didn't want anyone to see them."

"Yep." Jack sighed. "He said he didn't want anyone

to know about his condition because he was afraid it would negatively impact people's perceptions of him as a writer. He's afraid that if people think no more books are coming, sales will dry up."

"I feel sorry for the guy now," Ida said. All heads swiveled to look at her. Ida wasn't usually the type to feel sorry for people. "But that still doesn't explain why he was so interested in Mary's book."

"We asked him about that too," Jack said. "Bennington claimed he wanted to see one of his signed copies again since he can't sign books anymore."

"Oh. That's kind of sad." Lexy reluctantly crossed Chandler Bennington off her suspect list. Now she felt sorry for him too.

"And that's why he argued with Lorelei and refused to sign the books in her shop. It wasn't that he didn't want to. He couldn't. Oh, and I also reviewed the bartender's testimony. He was able to confirm that Chandler sat at the bar the whole time," Jack said. "So, I'm sorry to say that it wasn't him."

"See." Ida's voice had that I-told-you-so tone to it. "Like I said right off the bat, it's usually the husband. I knew it was Howard!"

"At dinner the other night, Lexy mentioned the gift Howard Archer was seen carrying around, so I did some checking on that." Jack riffled through his notes.

Lexy's heart swelled. He'd taken her clues seriously this time and actually acted on them. If that wasn't true love, she didn't know what was.

"Turns out Howard had purchased a pair of emerald earrings at the local jewelry store."

"Emeralds, eh?" Helen frowned. "Was Mary wearing them when you found her, Lexy?"

Lexy thought back to that day in the pie room. "I don't think so. I'm not sure I noticed." Dang! She should be more observant about things like that. Lexy glanced at Jack.

"That's right; she was wearing gold hoops," Jack said.

"Well, that makes no sense at all," Helen said. "If my man gave me an expensive gift like that, I'd open it right away and wear it for everyone to see. Especially if it came in a tiny box from the jewelry store."

"Me too," Ruth said. "When Nunzio used to give me jewelry, I'd rip it open right in the restaurant and put it on right away. It's kind of rude not to."

"Agreed," Nans said. "Which means Mary most likely never opened that gift."

"Or it was never meant for her. My suspicion is that Howard bought those earrings for someone else," Jack said, sitting back again to clasp his hands behind his head. "The question is ... who?"

"Sylvia did hint that Howard and Mary didn't get along," Lexy said.

"Well, if Howard is the killer, we're back to square one," Nans said. "That would mean Mary's death had nothing to do with that book and she died because Howard wanted to get rid of her."

"A crime of passion," Ida said, her voice brimming with excitement.

Helen and Ruth both rolled their eyes.

"There was something else Sylvia mentioned," Nans said. "That Howard had purchased an insurance policy from Dottie Smith's son. Maybe he had a double motive for wanting Mary dead."

Jack made another note. "I'll follow up on that."

"Perfect." Nans stood and headed for the door with the rest of the ladies in tow. "We'll just head back to my apartment for tea, then."

CHAPTER EIGHTEEN

"Can we stop for a snack to bring back to your place along the way?" Ida asked as they piled into Lexy's VW. "It's been a few hours since lunch, and I'm feeling peckish."

"When aren't you hungry?" Ruth snorted.

"I have an extra string cheese in my purse," Helen offered. "Want me to dig it out for you?"

"No." Ida gave her a look. "I want real food."

"Enough," Nans said. "We're not going back to my apartment anyway."

"We're not?" Lexy asked. "That's what you told Jack."

Nans slid a glance at Lexy from the passenger seat. "That's just what I told him because I didn't want him to feel like we were taking over the investigation. For once, he seems happy to cooperate with us, and I want to keep it that way."

"Yeah. We don't need him closing us out because he feels like we're finding all the clues before the cops," Ida said.

"That's right. We need to make them feel like *they* have a good handle on the investigation and that *we* are depending on *them*." A smile crept across Nans's lips. "Even though we know it's really the other way around."

Lexy wasn't so sure about that. Jack was a darn good detective, though it did seem she and the ladies were coming up with more clues. Somehow, she had a feeling Jack was letting them feel that way. He was probably one step ahead of them but making *them* feel as if they were ahead. "So where are we going, then?"

"Dottie Smith's place, of course. We need to find out about that insurance policy Howard bought from her grandson. It's better that we ask her. I'm sure she wouldn't want to get her grandson in trouble by giving out any insurance information to the cops, but I bet she'll spill her guts to us."

"I just hope Jack doesn't get angry if he thinks we went there before—" Lexy halted as a silver Toyota Camry turned the corner. Lorelei Summers was behind the wheel. She looked at them in surprise, her eyes darting from their faces to the police station they'd just left, before speeding away. "Well, that was odd. Why would she close up her store in the middle of a busy afternoon?"

"Why indeed." Nans stared after Lorelei's car. "Dottie lives in Building C right across the parking lot from my place. And if you are worried, Lexy, Jack doesn't need to know. You know how slow the police are to do anything. If we hurry, we can interrogate Dottie and be out of there before Jack gets there. We need to find out exactly how much that insurance policy was for. It could be the prime motive for Mary's murder."

Lexy parked in the middle lot in between Nans's building and Building C, and they all piled out to walk along the sidewalk to Dottie's building. The large glass doors opened to a lobby just like the one in Nans's building, with comfortable sofas, a big-screen television, and a few large round tables where residents could congregate. The same indoor-outdoor carpeting lined the hallways. Ruth knew the apartment number and knocked on the door.

Dottie was in her late seventies and had curly white hair and a pleasant smile that widened upon seeing them in the hall.

"Ladies, what a nice surprise." Dottie ushered

them inside. "How lovely of you to visit. I hardly ever see you anymore, Ruth."

"Yes, I'm sorry about that, Dottie. Been meaning to get over to visit. Hope you've been well."

"Indeed, I have." Dottie's apartment was a different model from Nans's, larger, with a living room off to the left and a kitchen open to a dining room on the right. It was loaded with potted plants and smelled of cinnamon cookies. Lexy could practically see Ida's nose twitching at the delicious scent.

Dottie raised her white brows. "Tea and cookies?"

"We'd love some." Ida practically bowled the woman over on her way to the kitchen.

They took seats at Dottie's breakfast bar. Lexy admired the kitchen while Dottie busied herself gathering the tea and cookies. It looked as though it had been recently renovated. Off-white cabinets with nice paneled details, shiny black granite, stainless steel appliances. *Maybe I should think about upgrading,* Nans thought.

"We don't want you to go to any trouble," she said. "We just wanted to chat about a few things."

"No trouble at all. I love having visitors." Dottie set a plate of cookies, a basket of tea bags, and a steaming kettle on the bar in front of them and took a seat while they loaded their plates. "So what did you want to talk about?"

"Oh, well, as you know, my granddaughter, Lexy, catered the book club gala." Nans selected a tea bag from the basket, took it out of the packet, and put it in her cup.

"Yes, she did a fine job." Dottie smiled at Lexy. "Terrible thing that happened, though, with Mary."

"Right." Nans poured steaming water into her cup. "The investigation is still ongoing, and well ... I thought it might help Lexy if we could try to figure out who would do that to Mary. You know, so it doesn't hurt Lexy's business."

This wasn't the first time Nans had used Lexy as an excuse to get information. Lexy didn't mind, though she did wish Nans would ask ahead of time. But playing on people's sympathies by pretending her business was in jeopardy usually worked, so she remained silent.

"Oh, of course. I didn't realize the murder had anything to do with Lexy's catering," Dottie said.

"It doesn't." Nans pulled the tea bag out by its cardboard tab and wrapped it around her spoon, squeezing the golden water back into the cup. "But still, Lexy is my only grandchild, and you know how we grandmothers are. I don't want there to be any blemishes on her events."

Dottie brightened. "Oh, I sure do. Why, my grandson, Tommy, is the light of my life. I'd do anything to help him in his new career. He's selling insurance, you know."

"I heard." Nans raised a brow at the ladies, who were busy scarfing down cookies. Well, except for Helen—she was dipping her string cheese in her tea.

Lexy was impressed. Nans had segued into the subject perfectly.

"But I don't think I can be much help. I was sitting at the table in the back the whole time and didn't see a thing," Dottie said.

"I think you might be able to help in another way," Nans said. "Sylvia Hensel said that Tommy sold Howard a life insurance policy. We were wondering if you knew anything about it."

"Oh yes. It was one of his first sales. That Howard is such a nice man. He wanted to help Tommy out. You know that if they make so many sales, they get bumped up in commission rate."

Nans nodded. "Uh-huh. And I bet if the policy is worth a lot, they do too, right?"

"Oh yes."

"And was Howard's worth a lot?"

Dottie frowned. "I don't think so. Just enough so Mary wouldn't be destitute."

The ladies exchanged confused glances.

"What do you mean, 'so Mary wouldn't be destitute'?" Ruth asked. "Wasn't the policy on Mary?"

"Oh no. It was on Howard." Dottie bit her lower lip. "Oh, I'm probably not supposed to be telling anyone this. Isn't it confidential or something? I don't want to get Tommy in trouble."

"No. I don't think so." Nans looked at the others.

"Nope." Ruth said.

"I'm pretty sure you can tell anyone. It's not like hiring a lawyer. It's just insurance." Ida took another cookie.

"Oh, okay. Well, the policy wasn't on Mary. I'm guessing Howard probably knew what was coming." Dottie looked down at her tea.

"What do you mean?" Nans scowled.

"Well, it's sad. When a person starts to lose their mind, their health suffers too. I'm sure he wanted to make sure he didn't leave Mary with nothing," Dottie said.

Lexy exchanged a look with Nans. "Are you saying that Howard Archer is ill?"

Dottie nodded. "Early stages of dementia, I think."

"How do you know that?" Helen asked.

"Well, by the way he was acting." Dottie looked at them as if they should all know. "I mean, it was quite obvious."

Lexy glanced at the others. From the blank looks on their faces, she knew it was not obvious to any of them.

"Could you be more specific?" Nans asked. "What made it obvious?"

"He did strange things. Like the night of the party, right before Lexy's announcement." Dottie shook her head. "I saw Howard, as plain as day, rummaging around in the coat closet at the community center."

"That's hardly reason to think someone's losing their mind," Ida said.

"No, but it is odd." Dottie lifted her chin. "It's eighty degrees outside and the middle of summer. Nobody's wearing coats."

CHAPTER NINETEEN

"So, Howard must have been searching the closet for something at the time Mary died," Helen said as they exited the building and started along the sidewalk toward Nans's apartment. The midafternoon sun had heated the day to the mideighties, and the warmth was causing the ladies to break into a sweat even though the sidewalk was partially shaded by tall oaks.

"But does that clear him of the murder?" Ida asked.

"Hmm. That's a good question. We need to think about the timing. Maybe he was ducking into the closet to hide after killing her," Lexy suggested.

"You're probably right. Why else would he have lied about being at the poker game that whole time?" Ruth asked.

LEIGHANN DOBBS

Ida snorted. "Yeah, I figure it would be the husband. Maybe he was after the book and hid it in the closet."

Helen frowned. "Why would he need to do that? Sylvia said Mary always had the key. I'm sure Howard could have gotten his hands on it some other time and taken the book, probably without her even knowing."

"Maybe he did that, but Mary found out," Lexy suggested. "Maybe that's what the fight was about. It turned ugly, and he killed her."

"Wait, I'm confused," Ruth said. "Was Howard after the book, or did he want to get rid of Mary because he was having an affair?"

"Maybe both," Ida suggested. "He might have wanted some quick money from the book to buy more gifts for his girlfriend."

"Maybe we should be trying to figure out who the girlfriend is," Helen suggested.

"And why did he take an insurance policy out on himself?" Nans asked.

"There're a lot of questions," Lexy said. "But first I think we need to figure out for sure if being in the closet eliminates him as a suspect."

"Right." Nans slowed, her lips pursing as she thought. "My biggest concern is our list of suspects.

Chandler has been cleared, and now Dottie might be Howard's alibi. So who does that leave as suspects?"

Lexy's mind returned to the weird conversation they'd had earlier in the antiques store. "Lorelei!"

"How so?" Ida asked.

"If we go back to our original theory that Mary was killed because of the book's value, then she would be a prime suspect," Lexy said.

They'd stopped walking and stood in a circle under the shade of a tall oak. A breeze blew the crisp smell of earth and freshly cut grass toward them. Under the tree, a squirrel dug for acorns. Above, birds hopped in the branches.

Ruth brushed a blue-tinged curl out of her eye. "I don't know. She said she doesn't use the Internet and had no idea how much that book was worth. Everyone thought it was worthless until we found it on eBay, but if she doesn't scour eBay, then how would she know?"

"Humph. People lie all the time, especially if they are killers," Ida said. "And she could have found out the value from any of her antiques-dealer friends. They all talk about such things."

"And that would explain the dirty look she gave us at the corner," Lexy said.

"No one saw her in the hallway," Helen pointed out. "But if you want to explore that option, then

Sylvia should be able to corroborate her alibi about helping with those bibs by the front door. Funny, though, that Sylvia didn't mention anything about being up in the front lobby to us when we spoke with her. You might be onto something, Lexy."

"Lorelei might have lied about the timing of helping Sylvia with the bibs to provide herself with an alibi."

"It would be pretty dumb for Lorelei to lie about that given that Sylvia could blow it out of the water," Ida said.

"She was probably hoping that Sylvia would be so discombobulated that she wouldn't remember," Nans said.

"It's possible Sylvia went to get those bibs after she talked to Chandler. Then I suppose it makes sense. But Lorelei could've still killed Mary and then rushed to the front door afterward," Lexy said.

"But how would she have gotten out of the pie room without being seen?" Nans started walking, but instead of heading for the glass doors of her building, she turned toward the parking lot, making a beeline for Lexy's VW. "We need to take another look at the pie room and talk to Sylvia again. I think we're homing in on something, and I want to double- and triple-check."

Lexy remembered her promise to Jack. They'd

filled him in earlier in the day. Surely that counted toward keeping him informed. And because their suspects wouldn't be at the community center, she wasn't heading into danger. She fished her keys from her purse and jogged up to Nans. "Good idea; get our theory straight, and then we can fill Jack in."

"Of course, dear. We don't want to flub up again. He's already disproved our theory about Chandler Bennington being the killer. We don't want to be wrong again. Besides, I'm working on a hunch that just might prove who could have done it and how."

CHAPTER TWENTY

*T*he community center parking lot was empty, the building locked. They peeked through the windows but couldn't see anyone inside.

"Anyone have their card handy?" Nans asked.

"I do." Helen stepped forward to slide her plastic card through the reader.

The automatic doors hissed open, and they walked inside. The place was quiet and still.

"I wonder where Sylvia is," Ida said.

"Maybe she went out for an errand," Ruth suggested. "Must be difficult now with no president. It's really just the president and treasurer who come to the offices, and with one person, I imagine Sylvia can't be here all the time."

Ida shrugged. "It's not necessary anyway. Ever

175

since we voted to get rid of having a security person all the time, we can use our cards to get in."

"Yeah, but Helen didn't like it much. I think she was sweet on that guy Sam who used to come on Tuesday and Thursday."

"I was not!" Helen's voice was sharp with conviction, but the wistful glance she shot toward the closed security door said otherwise.

Ida looked in through the glass window on top of the door, getting close to the glass and cupping her hands around her eyes. "Too bad they were too cheap to keep up with the security tapes. Look at all these monitors." She gestured toward the window, and Lexy peered inside.

The room was dimly lit. Several monitors lined a small desk, green lights glowing on the lower left to indicate they were "on." The monitors and cameras worked. They just didn't record what was happening. If someone wanted to, they could sit in the room and watch what was going on in different areas of the center in real time. Too bad no one was sitting there the night Mary was killed.

The room was only about ten by ten. Beige metal filing cabinets lined one wall. A gray metal desk hulked in the middle. One wall contained a giant corkboard that must have been left over from the security guard days. It still had a schedule tacked up, along with various index cards, an envelope with what looked like time cards, a key dangling from a green ribbon, several key cards like the kind Helen had used to open the door, and the old badges of the former security guards, including Sam, the one Helen had been interested in.

"Security footage and on-site guards are very expensive." Helen had come to stand beside Lexy and was also looking into the room, her eyes scanning the contents and coming to rest on Sam's badge. "The community center can only afford so much. You don't want your homeowners association fees to go up now, do you?"

"I suppose not."

"And besides, nothing ever really happens where we needed to review the footage," Helen added.

"Yeah, until now, right, Mona?" Ida turned around when Nans didn't answer. "Mona?"

Nans wasn't paying attention to the conversation. She'd stepped past the foyer into the main function room, where they'd set up the tables for the party. They joined her in the room. She stood in the center, a quizzical look on her face.

"Something wrong?" Lexy asked.

Nans held up a finger, and Lexy, Ruth, Ida, and

Helen exchanged a raised-brow glance. They followed her as she walked to the area where they'd set up the bar, checked her watch, spun on her heel, and walked to the hallway before checking her watch again.

"It's just the timing. How did the killer get down the hallway without being seen? There's no exit down at the end where the offices are." Nans tapped her lips with her index finger. "But I have an idea."

They followed Nans down the hall to the pie room. The police had finished processing the room. The long tables Lexy had set up for the contest were gone, as were the stained white linen tablecloths. No crime scene tape or fingerprint dust was present to remind anyone that a murder had been committed here.

"Mona, the police have gone over this room a dozen times. I'm pretty sure Jack knows what he's doing. You're not going to find anything that he didn't find," Ida said.

"And we scoured it ourselves that very day," Helen added.

Nans stared at the windows. She had that look on her face, like a beagle on the scent of a fox. When she got that look, it usually meant that she was on to something. She marched over to one of the windows and tugged. It didn't budge.

"Mona, what are you doing? You know we keep these locked up tight." Ida tugged on the window next to her to prove her point, and it slid up a half inch. She glanced down at it. "Well, I'll be a monkey's uncle."

"Aha! Just as I thought," Nans said. "You see? Sometimes the clue isn't something you find lying around. It's something that's not the norm. Like the window. Normally, Mary was a stickler for them being locked."

"That's true," Lexy said. "I wanted to crack them to cool the pies near the window. Even though it's hot out, the breeze and fresh air add to the taste somehow. But she wouldn't let me open them."

Nans nodded. "Of course. And didn't Jack say he didn't know how the pies could cool *despite the hot air outside*? Why would he say that if they weren't in the open window? The center is air conditioned."

"Are you thinking what I'm thinking?" Ruth asked.

"That someone deliberately opened that window to escape?" Nans asked. "Yes."

Lexy pushed the cracked window higher to look out. "Well, whoever it was knocked the screen out too. It's lying on the ground there, in the grass."

"So, Mary's killer tried to escape fast and leave through the window to avoid being seen. He knocked out the screen, climbed through, then drew the curtains and shut the window behind him."

"Except he couldn't shut it all the way because his fingers were in the way." Lexy stood back and looked at the curtains. "I think I might have even seen the curtains moving when I found Mary, but then I was so startled by the body I didn't think twice."

"Either the killer must've forgotten to replace the screen, or they didn't have time because Lexy and Cassie came in and discovered Mary's body," Ida said.

Nans walked to the area where Mary's body had been then pantomimed the motions the killer would've taken, timing it on her watch as she went. "The killer clonked Mary on the head with the trophy, which Mary had with her." She frowned. "Lexy, when you first saw Mary's body, was there a sign of struggle? Did it look as if she'd fought back?"

"No. She was facedown in a blueberry pie," Lexy said. "Then when I tapped her shoulder, she fell over onto the floor. Now that I think about it, it was weird that she was sitting down, right? I mean why would she be? The contest hadn't started yet. And it was dark in here."

"Right." Nans stepped back. "So, I'm guessing the murderer killed her then put her in the chair after he hit her over the head, perhaps to buy time. Did Jack mention that?"

Lexy frowned. "No."

"Surely the police would know if the body was moved," Ruth said.

"Of course they would. But sometimes Jack doesn't let everything out. Not even to us, apparently." Nans sighed. "I suppose we can't expect him to. He can't risk certain things getting out to the public, or it might prevent them from tripping the killer up in an interrogation. But that's okay. We don't need to know everything. We can still solve this case."

Lexy was still frowning. She felt a bit betrayed that Jack hadn't told her. Then again, Nans was right. And she supposed it didn't matter to their civilian investigation if they knew the body had been moved. Still, it felt like a lie, and it stung. Lexy pushed those feelings aside. This wasn't personal; it was Jack's job, and catching a killer was at stake. Besides, Jack *had* shared more than ever with her on this case.

"Okay. But if we're going with the book as motive, then the killer would have had to get the key from around Mary's neck, run to the office, get the book from the safe, run back, and escape through the window before anyone saw and before Lexy and Cassie arrived. Would he have had time?" Ruth asked.

"Let's find out." Nans followed the path from where Mary's body had been found, across the hall to Mary's office. Ruth was beside her, timing it all. The rest of them tagged along.

Mary's office wasn't the tidy place it had been when they'd first visited. Apparently, Sylvia had taken over, and if the condition of her own office was any indication, she wasn't nearly as neat as Mary had been. Papers were scattered. One stack in particular leaned askew, precariously close to the edge, a blue ribbon sticking out from beneath. Apparently, now with Mary gone, no one was overly worried about leaving the keys lying around.

"So, the killer must have known Mary wore the key around her neck. Wouldn't take but a second to get that as he put her body in the chair. He raced from the pie room to the office, unlocked the safe, took the book, closed the safe, ran back to the pie room, and climbed out the window."

Nans raced forward once more, the rest of the ladies hurrying behind her. "If it was Lorelei Summers, she'd have had to run around to the front door to meet Sylvia." She glanced at Ruth, who clicked the button on her stopwatch.

"Seven minutes. Might be enough time, if she'd

managed to hit Mary hard enough with the first blow of that trophy to kill her immediately."

"And whoever it was just sauntered in the front door like nothing happened?" Lexy asked.

"Good question." Helen raised a brow. "That might explain why Lorelei was helping Sylvia with the bibs near the front. She'd just snuck in the front door."

"The killer must have hidden the book too, because no one mentioned seeing it inside the community center again. Maybe we should check outside. It could be hidden in the bushes somewhere," Ida said.

"I doubt it would still be there," Nans said. "The value of a book decreases dramatically if it has damage. The killer wouldn't want it exposed to the elements. He probably stashed it somewhere inside."

Ida snorted. "Like where?"

"The closet," Nans said. "Dottie said she saw Howard rooting around in there right before Lexy made the announcement about the contest. Perhaps he wasn't looking for something. He might have been hiding something."

"The closet is right next to the front door," Ruth pointed out.

"Wait. So now you think Howard is the killer?" Helen asked.

LEIGHANN DOBBS

"Haven't ruled him out yet," Ida said. "And he couldn't easily climb out the window."

"Exactly!" Nans narrowed her gaze. "It still feels like we're missing a piece of the puzzle here, though. Now that we know more, let's run through the whole thing from start to finish. Ida, you can be the one to climb out the window just like the killer did."

Before they could begin, a voice from the hallway startled them.

"Excuse me, ladies. I'm here to confess to the murder of Mary Archer."

CHAPTER TWENTY-ONE

They wheeled to see Lorelei Summers standing in the doorway. She shuffled nervously, the wide sleeves of her loose purple shirt fluttering as she wrung her hands. Her face was lined with stress, her silver hair pulled back in a ponytail, green gems glittering in her lobes.

Nans was the first to recover from the shock. She frowned and stepped forward. "Did you say you're confessing to Mary Archer's murder?"

"Yes." Lorelei stood stock-still, hands clasped in front of her, staring straight ahead as if facing down a firing squad. "I did it. I killed her."

"Really?" Nans's frown deepened as she glanced back at the rest of the ladies. "But why would you come here to confess? Shouldn't you go to the police?"

"I am, sort of." Lorelei pointed at Lexy. "She's married to that detective. And I saw all of you leaving the police station earlier when I drove by, so I know you're talking with him about the case, snooping around here and feeding him clues and such. When I saw Ruth's car outside, I figured this was as good a place as any to say my piece." She held out her wrists, as if she expected the women to slap a set of cuffs on her. "Go on. Take me in. I'm guilty."

Nans gave her a disbelieving stare. "I don't believe it. You had no reason to murder her. What was your motive?"

Lexy stared at Nans. One of their prime suspects had confessed, but Nans didn't seem convinced. She decided not to say anything, though. Nans usually knew what she was doing. Maybe this was some kind of reverse-psychology trick.

Lorelei gave a slight shrug. "Well, I just didn't like Mary, I suppose. She was always hanging around here like she owned the place and telling people what to do. And I guess I just got sick of it."

"Bah!" Ruth snorted. "She's the president of the community center. She's supposed to tell people what to do. Besides, from what I've seen, the two of you got along just fine."

"It's called acting. I played nice with her while she

was around so no one would suspect that I couldn't stand her." Lorelei rolled her eyes. "I'd think after all the time you spent hanging around with mobsters, you'd know a bit about covering up."

"Why, you..." Ruth advanced on Lorelei with a scowl. "I ought to pop you a good one. And here I always thought you were a nice person."

"People can fool you," Lorelei said, though her tone lacked conviction.

Nans held up a hand, gaze narrowed. "So, you're telling us that you killed Mary, took the book for the contest, ran down the hallway, and hid it in the coat closet, all without being seen?"

Eyes wide, Lorelei nodded. "That's exactly what happened. Everyone knows they don't tape around here, so I didn't have to worry about the security cameras. And there were so many people at the party it was easy to do what I needed with all the distractions."

"And what did you do with the key?" Ida asked, moving in beside Nans and crowding Lorelei.

"Um..." Lorelei's confident expression faltered. "Uh, I tossed it in the garbage."

And the book?" Nans persisted. "Where is it now?"

"I sold it."

Nans looked at her skeptically. "Really? When we were at your shop earlier, you didn't seem to care much at all about it. You said you don't even have Internet access, so you only keep them around for the tourists."

"You said it was valuable, so I took it and sold it," Lorelei said, raising her chin.

Ruth, Ida, and Helen exchanged confused looks. Lorelei was lying about something, but why?

"Yes, but you didn't find out that it was valuable until today. Mary's death was two days ago," Nans stepped closer to Lorelei and looked at her ears. "Are those emerald earrings?"

Lorelei reached up and covered her lobes with her hands. "Maybe. I don't know. Why? What about them? Look, I just confessed to a murder. Shouldn't one of you be calling the police or something? I'm ready to be taken into custody." She reached into her pocket and pulled out a slim recorder. "See? I've even recorded my confession for you. Doesn't get any easier than that, ladies."

"Nope." Nans sighed and shook her head. "No one's arresting you today, Lorelei. I'd say the only thing you're guilty of is fooling around with a married man."

Lorelei gasped. "How dare you make such an accusation!"

Ruth snorted again. "So, you're fine with being

charged with murder, but call you an adulteress, and you've got a problem with it? Makes no sense at all."

"I knew there was something about those earrings," Helen said, her tone full of pride. "That's the gift Howard was carrying around at the party. They were for you, weren't they?"

Lorelei's cheeks flushed an unflattering shade of red. "Fine. Yes! It's true. Howard and I are having an affair. I killed Mary so I could have him all to myself."

The clues from the case ran through Lexy's head, and a few pieces clicked together. "What were you and Howard fighting about at the party?"

"Blast it!" Lorelei's brave façade crumbled, and tears streamed down her face. "He said I stood him up, but I never did. I wouldn't." She sniffled and swiped the back of her hands across her damp cheeks. "But I would kill for him. I would."

"Sorry, Lorelei," Nans said. "But I'm not buying it. You're not the killer."

"But I'm confessing!" Lorelei cried in frustration.

"No dice. Earlier when I asked what happened, you said you killed Mary and ran down the hallway and put the book in the closet. Are you sure that's what happened?"

Lorelei looked around at all of them—Nans with her brows up, Ida with her arms crossed, foot tapping,

Helen with her hands on her hips, Ruth with her head cocked to the side, awaiting the answer. "Yes, that's right. But Howard had no idea I was hiding the book in the closet. I swear."

Nans shook her head. "Nope. Sorry. The killer didn't run down the hallway. The killer went out the window. You would have known that if you were the real killer."

"You're just covering for Howard," Ida said. "We have witnesses who saw him near the closet just before Mary's body was discovered."

"No!" Lorelei stamped her foot, but the effect was lost on the carpeted floor. "Howard Archer did not kill his wife. It was me. I swear! I won't let Howard go to jail for this. He had nothing to do with any of this. Howard's such a sweet man; he'd never survive in prison."

"Huh." Ida crossed her arms. "That's nice, but you still can't go to jail for a crime someone else committed."

"I can, and I will, if it saves him." Lorelei glared at them. "I can't live without Howard."

"Don't worry. Neither of you will have to live without the other. Because neither of you is going to jail," Nans said.

They all whipped their heads around to look at her.

"What do you mean?" Ida demanded.

"That's right. It's not Howard, and it's not Lorelei. But I know who it is." She pushed the pile of papers aside and picked up the pristine blue ribbon, letting the key dangle in the air in front of them. "There are only two keys to the safe. Mary had one around her neck, and presumably, the killer took it. Yet one is still hanging in the security office. And this ribbon is not stained with pie filling. Both keys have been here the whole time. Ladies, I hate to say it, but I think we got it slightly wrong."

Lorelei still looked confused although a bit more relieved now that neither she nor Howard was on Nans's list of suspects.

"Got it wrong? What do you mean?" Ida asked. "And if both keys were here the whole time, then what was the killer looking for in the pies?"

Nans started toward the door. "I don't have time to explain. Lexy, call Jack. We have to catch the killer before the evidence is destroyed!"

CHAPTER TWENTY-TWO

"Cut the lights and pull over here," Nans whispered a few minutes later as Lexy drove along one of the streets on the outskirts of the community center. It was dusk, and the street was bathed in shadows, but Lexy recognized Jack's car parked a few houses down. She coasted to a stop across from a small, cozy-looking bungalow. Nans had the door open almost before she stopped, and the ladies piled out.

Jack got out of his car and approached them, keeping his voice low. "Okay, ladies, I can handle this. We could be confronting a killer. I can't let civilians get hurt." He started toward the front door.

"Pffft..." Nans watched him walk to the door then turned to the rest of them. "If my guess is correct, we'll find the killer out back. Let's go."

LEIGHANN DOBBS

She hurried to the side of the house, Lexy and the others following. Lexy could smell the fire before they rounded the corner. In the middle of the yard, a stone fire pit blazed, orange flames licking at the darkening sky. A lone figure stood next to it, tossing papers into the fire.

"Destroying evidence?" Nans asked as she walked up to Sylvia Hensel.

Sylvia frowned at Nans then glanced at the rest of the women. "No. I'm just enjoying a bonfire. Is that a crime?"

"No." Jack appeared from the side of the house and grabbed a stick from the woodpile then used it to pull out the half-charred remnants of a book. "But interfering with a murder investigation certainly is."

"You killed Mary?" Ruth asked. "For a book?"

"I didn't kill anyone," Sylvia said, staring into the flames once more, her expression unreadable.

"Tell us what happened at the party, Sylvia." Lexy closed in on the other side of her. The heat from the fire prickled her skin. It was summer, after all, and a warm evening. "Tell us what you did that night."

"We already know you were in the office with Mary. I heard you," Helen said. "And you also lied about seeing Howard coming down the hall. He

194

couldn't have been there because he wasn't in the hall, was he? He was near the closet."

"I don't know. I thought I saw him, but with everything going on, I was confused," Sylvia said, her tone soft and tinged with sadness. "Maybe my timing was off."

"There was nothing wrong with your timing," Ida said. "You know why Howard was in that closet, don't you?"

"Of course she does." Nans smiled. "She's the one who slipped Howard a note telling him to meet Lorelei there."

"Really, Mona?" Ida turned to her friend. "How do you know that?"

"Easy enough, once I put all the clues together. Remembered the night of the party when we were all sitting there at the table and Sylvia came by and slipped that note under Howard's plate. We all saw it, but we thought it was something to do with the raffle."

"Yeah, I was still holding out for tickets to Cactus Joe's," Ida said.

"I remember a few of us even checked under our own plates to see if we had one too, but we didn't," Helen said. "I remember from the rules sheet Mary passed out prior to the party that there was supposed to have been one of those hidden notes present at every table. Then the raffle was canceled once the police arrived."

"That's right," Nans agreed. "But your note had nothing to do with the raffle, did it, Sylvia?"

Sylvia snorted and shook her head. "You have no proof of any of this."

"Oh, but I think we do." Nans pointed to Sylvia's pearls. "Your necklace and earrings. You always wear the pearls because they were your mother's. I've never seen you without them. But the other day, I noticed that you'd switched to wearing diamond earrings instead of the ones matching your necklace. Why is that, Sylvia? Could it be because you lost one of the pearl earrings? Say, maybe it fell off into the blueberry pie when you struggled with Mary."

Lexy stared at the diamonds twinkling in Sylvia's ears. Of course! How could she have missed it? Now she remembered that the day after Mary's death, they'd gone to talk to Sylvia, and she'd had the pearl necklace on but not the earrings.

"What?" Sylvia said, her tone incredulous.

"But we didn't find an earring in the pie," Jack said, frowning.

"No, I'm sure you didn't, because Sylvia retrieved it before you arrived." Nans sighed. "That's what the killer was digging for, not the key, like we'd thought."

Ida snapped her fingers. "Because the killer already had the key."

"That's right. Remember how you said your dentures stained something terrible when you ate blueberry pie?" Nans asked Ida.

Ida nodded.

"Well, pearls stain just as easily, and all that blueberry sauce would've been a nightmare. Sylvia couldn't wear that earring anymore." Nans raised a brow at Sylvia. "Could you?"

Sylvia's eyes darted between Nans and the ladies before turning to Jack.

"And the key that Mary wore around her neck—she wasn't wearing it that night, was she? It would have clashed with her pink outfit. And it had no pie stains on it. She had probably entrusted it to you." Nans pointed at Sylvia.

"You're wrong." Sylvia sounded tired, as if she knew she'd been caught and was just going through the motions.

"Jack, I'm sure that if you get a warrant to inspect the interior of Sylvia's house, you'll find all the proof you need." She glanced down at the still-smoldering book at Jack's feet. "Plus, she was burning evidence."

"But why would she burn something so valuable?" Helen asked.

"The copy of Chandler Bennington's book that Mary bought at the rummage sale was long gone by the night of the party. This one was a fake. The original copy was the one we found sold on eBay."

"But that auction took place weeks ago," Ruth said.

"Yes, right after Mary had first bragged about her purchase around the community center, claiming she'd discovered a real treasure with Bennington's authentic signature. The one Sylvia tried to burn tonight is the one she forged. That's why she needed it gone."

"Sorry, I'm not following any of this," Ida said.

"Don't you see?" Nans turned to face the group. "It makes perfect sense. The only person who would know whether or not the signature in that book was authentic was Chandler himself. Things were going fine for Sylvia until Mary convinced Chandler to come to the center to award the winner the prize of his signed book. But by that time, Sylvia had already stolen the original from the safe and replaced it with the fake. The signature made it valuable. No one else here, not even Lorelei, had any idea how much the original book was actually worth, so they wouldn't look too closely. It wouldn't have mattered. But Chandler's arrival changed everything. That's why Sylvia was so uncooperative when Chandler wanted to see the book. I'm guessing Sylvia was thinking perhaps she could destroy it or damage it badly enough before the contest that it couldn't have been used as a prize. But then circumstances prevented that from happening, and she had to turn to desperate measures to keep Chandler from seeing it after the contest. He would've known immediately that his signature had been forged."

"It was a good plan too. It would have worked," Sylvia said, her words hushed by the crackle of the fire. "Trying to eke out a living on Social Security is hard. I have expensive taste. That book was just sitting there in Mary's safe, collecting dust." She blinked slowly, her face illuminated in dancing shades of orange and yellow. "Mary didn't care one whit about it, other than bragging rights for finding it in the first place. She doesn't even like to read cozy mysteries. So yes, I took it, and I sold it. All I wanted was a little extra money, a little more to back up my savings and have to spend for a rainy day. I never meant to hurt anyone." Tears welled in her eyes, reflecting the fire's glow. "I never intended to kill Mary. I was just trying to talk her into giving another prize besides the book."

"A voucher for Cactus Joe's would have been good," Ida muttered.

Sylvia continued, "But she wouldn't do it. Lucky

for me, she carried along that stupid, worthless trophy. The contest was scheduled to start soon, and I couldn't be seen. I grabbed the nearest thing I could find in the dark and hit Mary over the head with it to knock her out. I was going to pretend someone stole the book." She squeezed her eyes shut. "I didn't think I'd hit her that hard. But then she wouldn't wake up, so I pulled the book from her hands and dragged her into a seat. Good thing I work out—she was heavy. My earring fell out in the melee, and I had to waste time digging for it through all those blueberries. I barely had time to shimmy out the window and close it again after me before Lexy walked in and found Mary." Sylvia hiccupped on a sob. "I'm so sorry. I'm so sorry to Mary and to all of you. I'm so, so sorry."

Jack dropped his stick then and moved forward, unclipping the set of handcuffs attached to his belt. "Sylvia Hensel, you're under arrest for the murder of Mary Archer. You have the right to remain silent. Anything you say can and will be used against you in a court of law..."

As Jack read Sylvia her rights, Lexy turned back to Nans, who was watching the action with the other ladies.

"Go figure," Ida said, shaking her head. "It wasn't the key that was in the pie, but an earring."

Nans sighed. "I knew something wasn't right when I saw that key in Mary's office when we did our walk-through at the center earlier. It wasn't until later that I realized Sylvia was the only person with access to both keys besides Mary. And we'd seen the key hanging on the ribbon in the security office earlier, so Mary's key actually wasn't ever missing. Sylvia had it the whole time."

"And she could have accessed the safe at any time. I'm sure Mary would give her the key, or she could have used the one from the security office," Helen said. "So she could have removed the book and replaced it with the fake at any time. No one would be the wiser."

"When Lorelei confessed and we discovered her wearing the earrings Howard had given her, it got me thinking about how Sylvia hadn't been wearing the pearl earrings that matched her necklace, even though she loved them." Nans continued, "It hit me—if Sylvia had been wearing those pearl earrings at the party and one of them had been damaged, say by falling into a blueberry pie during her struggle with Mary in the pie room, that would've been quite a mess."

"Just like my dentures," Ida said.

"Yep." Nans laughed. "The same thing would have happened to Sylvia's pearls."

"Well, another case solved by the Ladies' Detective Club." Ida held her fist out, and all the ladies bumped it as Jack escorted Sylvia away.

"Hey, Jack," Nans yelled just before he disappeared around the side of the house, causing him to turn and look at her. "Throw the book at her!"

CHAPTER TWENTY-THREE

*T*he next morning, Lexy and Cassie were in the kitchen of The Cup and Cake just after the morning rush.

"So, Nans and the ladies solved another case." Cassie opened the oven, and the sugary scent of almond scones wafted out.

"Yeah, but don't say it that way to John. Jack thinks they solved it." Lexy picked up an éclair, careful not to touch the chocolate icing dripping down the sides as she placed it next to another éclair on the doily-covered stand.

Cassie laughed. "They always do."

"I'm sure they helped," Lexy joked as she placed the last éclair on the stand. "Nans just has a slight advantage because she can talk to people on a different

203

level. They tend to clam up when the cops ask questions. Anyway, I know Jack and John would have figured it out, but Nans had some information just a bit sooner than they did."

"It seems like Jack didn't mind you investigating this time." Cassie gently slid the scones from the baking tray onto a wire rack to cool.

"I know, right? We shared clues and everything. Well, except for one clue that he held back. Then again, maybe I didn't fill him in as soon as I could have on everything Nans and I discovered, so I guess we're even." The bells over the door tinkled, and Lexy carefully picked up the stand with the éclairs on it. "I'll take care of this round of customers; you finish the baking."

Out front, Nans, Ruth, Ida, and Helen hovered in front of the bakery case. Outside, Ruth's blue Olds was precariously parked with its tires half on the sidewalk.

"Morning, ladies." Lexy slid the back door of the case open and nestled the stand between a platter of cannoli and a tiered stand filled with Danish.

"And a lovely morning it is." Nans gestured to indicate the sunny day outside. "It's always a good day when an investigation comes to a satisfactory conclusion."

"You can say that again," Ruth said.

"Sure is," Helen added.

"I'll take a cinnamon scone and a blonde brownie." Ida's gnarled index finger tapped the glass in front of the items she wanted.

Lexy pulled a bakery tissue from the box, grabbed Ida's items, and put them on one of the paper plates she kept for customers eating in-house. Nans ordered a blueberry muffin and pistachio biscotti, and Ruth ordered a snickerdoodle cookie and coffee cake. Lexy plated them all up before sliding the case door closed.

"Ahem." Helen stood in front of the case, a look of annoyance on her face. "I'll have a bear claw."

Lexy exchanged a surprised look with Nans and the other ladies then reopened the case and took out the pastry for Helen.

"Taking a break from your low-carb diet?" Ida asked Helen as they made their way toward the cafe tables.

"Nope. Gone off it completely." Apparently, Helen couldn't wait to get those carbs in, because she picked up the large pastry and took a big bite while she was still walking. "Did you know that it turns out a low-carb diet is actually bad for your health?"

"Really?" Ruth scrunched her nose and gave her friend a disbelieving look. "Everything I've read says it's quite healthy."

"Not in my case." Helen swallowed another bite of her enormous pastry. "I snuck into the kitchens for piecrust while a murderer was lurking about. I could've been killed!"

Ruth laughed, Ida snorted, and Nans shook her head.

"Let's sit outside." Nans pointed to the cafe tables on the sidewalk before heading to the coffee station. It was self-serve, but Lexy helped the ladies with their coffee, pouring the steaming brown liquid into the white ceramic mugs she kept on hand for patrons before pouring one for herself and heading out to the table, where Ida already had a napkin tucked into her blouse and was digging into her pastry.

The tables were shaded from the sun, making the midmorning temperature a perfect seventy-eight degrees. The faint sound of rushing water from the waterfall across the street made for relaxing background music. Nans broke off a small piece of her blueberry muffin and tossed it on the sidewalk. Two brown sparrows immediately swooped down to fight over it.

"That was some pretty spectacular detective work on your part, Nans," Lexy said over the rim of her coffee mug. "Especially the way you put it all together so quickly there at the end."

Nans shrugged, pulled off the top of her muffin,

and nibbled on the edge. "The apple doesn't fall far from the tree in our family. You have some pretty good powers of deduction yourself."

"And it doesn't hurt that you can use your powers of persuasion to get information out of Jack." Ida waggled her eyebrows.

"It was really a simple matter of deduction, although I almost missed the real clue," Nans said.

"What was that?" Lexy asked.

"Sylvia's earrings. I had noticed that she was wearing the diamonds instead of her usual pearls, and when someone mentioned that Howard bought Mary a small gift, it did cross my mind that the gift might have been those earrings. But Jack discovered that Howard bought emeralds before I could say anything about it. It wasn't until later that I realized Sylvia wasn't wearing the pearl earrings because one had fallen into the pie."

"Yeah, about those pies." Ida looked at Lexy. "Did Jack ever say what happened to them?"

"I'm afraid he had to throw them out," Lexy said.

Ida shook her head. "What a waste."

"Sylvia might have gotten away with the whole thing if Chandler Bennington hadn't agreed to come here and present the book," Ruth said.

"It's ironic because Mary had to try hard to talk

him into it, and it was such a coup for her to get him to come. She'd still be alive if she hadn't tried so hard," Helen said.

Nans tossed another small piece of her muffin to the birds. Now three were fighting over it. "Sylvia knew that Chandler would take one look at that book and know it was a fake. But one of her downfalls was that she told us she'd never talked to Chandler when in fact he'd contacted her a few times about the book. Remember he said she kept it locked up tighter than the Dead Sea Scrolls."

"And then she tried to set up poor Howard," Ida said, polishing off the last of her cinnamon scone before dusting the powdered sugar and cinnamon that had been sprinkled on top from her hands. "All to make the motive seem it was about getting Mary out of the way."

Ruth sniffed. "Yes. Poor Howard, misguided cheater that he was. She faked Lorelei's signature too, on that note she slipped under Howard's plate at the party."

Nans nodded. "Apparently, she knew all along about the two of them. She was trying to set him up so that he'd be in the closet alone and have no alibi. Lorelei didn't even know about the meeting, just as she said."

"She was very clever." Lexy reached over and pinched a tiny piece from the corner of Ida's blonde brownie, earning a dirty look from Ida. "She made all those insinuations when we questioned her about Howard but wasn't too obvious about it."

Ruth nodded. "And she never named Lorelei, knowing that if we figured it out on our own, it wouldn't be obvious that she was trying to manipulate us."

"It's too bad she's a killer," Nans said. "With a devious mind like that, she might make a good detective."

Ruth nodded. "True. She even included that little tidbit about the new life insurance policy to make it juicier. Talk about manipulation."

"Except she screwed up there." Ida moved her brownie farther from Lexy to discourage more pilfering. "She thought the policy was on Mary, but it was really on Howard."

"Turns out he just wanted to help out Dottie's grandson," Ruth said. "And I found out that he had no intention of divorcing Mary. He and Lorelei were happy with the way things were going. I kind of wish he turned out to be the killer. Can't stand a cheater."

Nans sighed. "Sylvia made another mistake. She never mentioned being at the front door with the bibs to us. Lorelei must have caught her just after she slipped back in, and she made the excuse that she was getting the bibs. She wouldn't want anyone to tell the police she'd been outside. But when we asked her, she simply said she had been tasked with talking to Chandler. She never mentioned the bibs because she probably didn't want to draw attention to the fact that she was near the door. I bet she told Jack the same story."

"I'm surprised she was flexible enough to climb out the window after killing Mary and then run around to the front of the center. But she didn't want to risk people saying they saw her come out from the hallway, so it was the only way. The police would never think a woman her age would climb out the window," Ruth said.

Ida scowled at Ruth. "Speak for yourself."

"We do have to admit she was very clever," Lexy said.

"But not as clever as us," Helen added.

"Well..." Ruth raised her coffee mug in a toast. "Congrats to us on another case solved."

"And for working together with Jack this time," Lexy added, clinking her cup with theirs.

"Yes," Nans said. "I hope we can work together with him more in the future."

Helen sat back from the table, brushing crumbs

from the front of her dress. "Guess it's back to the boring daily grind for now, eh?"

"I don't know about that," Ida said, her grin devious. "With Mary gone and Sylvia locked up, there's two new openings at the community center, and there's going to be an election. You know how cutthroat those can be. Could make for some good entertainment. Anyone interested in running?"

****

Sign up for my VIP reader list and get my books at the lowest discount price:
http://www.leighanndobbs.com/newsletter

Join my Facebook Readers group and get special content and the inside scoop on my books:
https://www.facebook.com/groups/ldobbsreaders

If you want to receive a text message on your cell phone for new releases, text COZYMYSTERY to 88202 (sorry, this only works for US cell phones!)

ALSO BY LEIGHANN DOBBS

Cozy Mysteries

Lexy Baker Cozy Mystery Series

* * *

Lexy Baker Cozy Mystery Series Boxed Set Vol 1 (Books 1-4)

Or buy the books separately:

Killer Cupcakes

Dying For Danish

Murder, Money and Marzipan

3 Bodies and a Biscotti

Brownies, Bodies & Bad Guys

Bake, Battle & Roll

Wedded Blintz

Scones, Skulls & Scams

Ice Cream Murder

Mummified Meringues

Brutal Brulee (Novella)

No Scone Unturned

Cream Puff Killer

Kate Diamond Mystery Adventures

***

Hidden Agemda (Book 1)

Ancient Hiss Story (Book 2)

Heist Society (Book 3)

Silver Hollow

Paranormal Cozy Mystery Series

***

A Spell of Trouble (Book 1)

Spell Disaster (Book 2)

Nothing to Croak About (Book 3)

Cry Wolf (Book 4)

Mooseamuck Island Cozy Mystery Series

* * *

A Zen For Murder

A Crabby Killer

A Treacherous Treasure

Mystic Notch

Cat Cozy Mystery Series

* * *

Ghostly Paws

A Spirited Tail

A Mew To A Kill

Paws and Effect

Probable Paws

Blackmoore Sisters

Cozy Mystery Series

* * *

Dead Wrong

Dead & Buried

Dead Tide

Buried Secrets

Deadly Intentions

A Grave Mistake

Spell Found

Fatal Fortune

Hazel Martin Historical Mystery Series

***

Murder at Lowry House (book 1)

Murder by Misunderstanding (book 2)

Lady Katherine Regency Mysteries

***

An Invitation to Murder (Book 1)

The Baffling Burglaries of Bath (Book 2)

Sam Mason Mysteries

(As L. A. Dobbs)

***

Telling Lies (Book 1)

Keeping Secrets (Book 2)

Exposing Truths (Book 3)

Betraying Trust (Book 4)

Contemporary Romance

***

Reluctant Romance

Sweet Romance (Written As Annie Dobbs)

Firefly Inn Series

***

Another Chance (Book 1)

Another Wish (Book 2)

Hometown Hearts Series

***

No Getting Over You (Book 1)

A Change of Heart (Book 2)

Romantic Comedy

***

Corporate Chaos Series

In Over Her Head (book 1)

Can't Stand the Heat (book 2)

What Goes Around Comes Around (book 3)

Careful What You Wish For (4)

***

Sweetrock Sweet and Spicy Cowboy Romance

Some Like It Hot

Too Close For Comfort

Regency Romance

* * *

Scandals and Spies Series:

Kissing The Enemy

Deceiving the Duke

Tempting the Rival

Charming the Spy

Pursuing the Traitor

Captivating the Captain

The Unexpected Series:

An Unexpected Proposal

An Unexpected Passion

Dobbs Fancytales:

Dobbs Fancytales Boxed Set Collection

Western Historical Romance

***

Goldwater Creek Mail Order Brides:

Faith

American Mail Order Brides Series:

Chevonne: Bride of Oklahoma

_____

Magical Romance with a Touch of Mystery

***

Something Magical

Curiously Enchanted

ROMANTIC SUSPENSE

WRITING AS LEE ANNE JONES:

***

The Rockford Security Series:

Deadly Betrayal (Book 1)

Fatal Games (Book 2)

Treacherous Seduction (Book 3)

Calculating Desires (Book 4)

Wicked Deception (Book 5)

ABOUT LEIGHANN DOBBS

USA Today bestselling author, Leighann Dobbs, discovered her passion for writing after a twenty year career as a software engineer. She lives in New Hampshire with her husband Bruce, their trusty Chihuahua mix Mojo and beautiful rescue cat, Kitty. When she's not reading, gardening, making jewelry or selling antiques, she likes to write cozy mystery and historical romance books.

Her book "Dead Wrong" won the "Best Mystery Romance" award at the 2014 Indie Romance Convention.

Her book "Ghostly Paws" was the 2015 Chanticleer Mystery & Mayhem First Place category winner in the Animal Mystery category.

Find out about her latest books by signing up at:

http://www.leighanndobbs.com/newsletter

Connect with Leighann on Facebook
http://facebook.com/leighanndobbsbooks

Join her VIP readers group on Facebook:
https://www.facebook.com/groups/ldobbsreaders
/

This is a work of fiction.

None of it is real. All names, places, and events are products of the author's imagination. Any resemblance to real names, places, or events are purely coincidental, and should not be construed as being real.

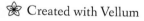